"What if I do or say the wrong thing?" Luc said hesitantly.

"Henry isn't my son yet. What if I do something that damages my case? What if I somehow hurt him or make a mistake with him? I couldn't stand that."

"Luc, nobody is born knowing how to be a parent. It's trial and error for everyone." Holly smiled, hoping to ease his anxiety. "Come on, Luc. You've talked about adopting Henry. Now's not the time to get cold feet. In fact, this is probably the perfect time to try the things you want to do with Henry when you adopt him. Show him what you love," she said quietly. "He'll love it, too."

"I guess that's my biggest fear," he admitted. "Maybe Henry won't like my life."

"Are you kidding? Cowboys are Henry's heroes. He's going to dive headlong into whatever you show him. But if he doesn't, you'll find something else, right? Because Henry is the son you've always wanted."

Without warning, Luc leaned forward and pressed a kiss against her forehead. "You're a good friend, Holly."

She gulped, utterly unnerved by that soft kiss and yet deeply moved that this strong, competent man needed her. It took a second to get her happy-go-lucky mask in place so Luc wouldn't see how deeply he'd affected her.

Lois Richer loves traveling, swimming and quilting, but mostly she loves writing stories that show God's boundless love for His precious children. As she says, "His love never changes or gives up. It's always waiting for me. My stories feature imperfect characters learning that love doesn't mean attaining perfection. Love is about keeping on keeping on." You can contact Lois via email, loisricher@yahoo.com, or on Facebook (LoisRicherAuthor).

Books by Lois Richer

Love Inspired

Family Ties

A Dad for Her Twins
Rancher Daddy

Northern Lights

North Country Hero
North Country Family
North Country Mom
North Country Dad

Healing Hearts

A Doctor's Vow
Yuletide Proposal
Perfectly Matched

Love for All Seasons

The Holiday Nanny
A Baby by Easter
A Family for Summer

Visit the Author Profile page at Harlequin.com
for more titles.

Rancher Daddy

Lois Richer

HARLEQUIN® LOVE INSPIRED®

Recycling programs
for this product may
not exist in your area.

LOVE INSPIRED BOOKS

ISBN-13: 978-0-373-04347-7

Rancher Daddy

www.Harlequin.com

Printed in U.S.A.

Let Him have all your worries and cares,
for He is always thinking about you and
watching everything that concerns you.
—*1 Peter* 5:7

This book is dedicated to children young and old who have ever felt abandoned, alone and unloved. You are not. God loves you with a love so deep no human love could touch it. If you let Him, He will fill your heart and soul so that you never again need to feel you're on your own.

Chapter One

Holly Janzen loved her early-morning ride home after a night shift on the hospital's pediatric ward. Especially now that spring had crept into the valley where Buffalo Gap nestled in the foothills of the Alberta Rocky Mountains. With the sun just cresting, the town lay bathed in the rosy hue of May's promise. The best part was that morning signaled a fresh start, untouched by the horrible memories of her past.

Holly gaped at the twenty-foot photo of her own face pasted to a huge billboard in the center of town, her heart sinking as she read,

Holly Janzen. Buffalo Gap's citizen of the year.

Why did they keep doing that? Several times a year Mayor Marsha Grant and the town council did something that featured Holly as the town's poster child for success. Years ago they'd granted Holly, the girl voted most likely to succeed, a scholarship to earn her nurse practitioner credentials in Toronto. The mayor and the rest of the town never heard the truth about those years down east and how un-poster-child-like she'd behaved, because nobody in Buffalo Gap ever saw past the good-girl image of her childhood. To them Holly Janzen was a role model they wanted their own kids to emulate.

As if!

Tired of the never-ending guilt that memories of those years in Toronto always brought, Holly shoved them away and focused instead on the sight of the newly renovated hotel that now housed Family Ties, an adoption agency two friends had set up to help kids who needed homes. But unlike most days, this morning Holly gave the place more than a yearning glance.

This morning a child sat on the steps that led to the front door.

A horn sounded behind her, a short beep, just enough to let her know someone didn't appreciate her pausing in the middle of the street. Holly identified the rusty brown half-ton truck in her rearview mirror and smiled. Luc Cramer, aka Mr. Just In Time.

Luc had come to her rescue many times but especially during her father's illness and after his death three months ago. He'd continued as Holly's ranch manager leaving her free to focus on her work as the community's nurse practitioner which often meant she helped pregnant moms deliver healthy newborns. A side benefit of that was that she got to work with moms-to-be at Family Ties.

Holly mostly accepted what Luc suggested in regard to the ranch and so far it was working out great. The only negative side was that whenever Holly voiced her concern that Luc wasn't benefitting as much as she was from the arrangement, he brushed her off.

Now Holly thrust her hand out of her car window, pointed to the boy on the steps then steered hard left, crossing the street to pull into an angled parking spot in front of Family Ties. Two seconds later Luc's truck pulled in beside hers as she jumped out of her orange jeep.

"Holly, you can't just stop in the middle of the street and then pull across it like that," he began in that quiet but pained tone he sometimes used, which carried a kind of big-brother resignation.

"What are you doing in town so early, Luc?" she asked.

"Just coming home from Calgary." He smiled at her arched eyebrow. "No, I wasn't partying, I was trying to help a friend who's going through a messy, painful divorce."

"That's nice of you." She tilted her head in the boy's direction. "Who's this little guy?"

"No idea. Let's find out." Luc followed Holly as she hurried forward. She was aware of him but her focus centered on the little boy in worn-out jeans and a tattered red hoodie sitting in front of Family Ties. Big black glasses made him look like a wise owl.

"Hi, honey," she said in a soft voice, crouching down to meet the child's gaze. "What's your name?"

"Henry." He blinked huge brown eyes at her then his gaze shifted to Luc. "Are you a real cowboy?" he asked in awed tones.

Holly turned to see Luc's slow, easy grin slash across his handsome, tanned face.

"Real as they get, partner," Luc said in a drawl that reminded her of some Hollywood star in a bygone Western movie. When he hunkered down beside Holly, his elbow brushed her arm, sending an electric charge up it as he thrust out a hand to shake Henry's.

Holly noticed the contact with her hunky foreman because it caused her stomach to do that shaky dance. But she couldn't figure out why that was. Luc was a friend but nothing more. That was the way she wanted it.

"Pleased to meet you, Henry. I'm Luc and that's Holly." Luc smiled then quietly asked, "What are you doing here?"

"Waiting." The boy reached up to touch the

brim of Luc's jet-black Stetson, the one Holly had only ever seen Luc remove for church and funerals. But this morning the cowboy took off his hat and set it on the boy's head. Henry's eyes widened. "I wish I had one of these."

"Maybe one day you will." Luc shot Holly a look that asked for help.

She nodded. They needed to find out more about this boy so they could figure out what to do next.

"Are you waiting for someone special, Henry?" Holly asked.

"Uh-huh. The people who work here." The boy jerked a thumb over one shoulder. "They find families for kids. I want one."

Nonplussed, Holly glanced at Luc, who stared right back at her, his brown eyes crinkling at the corners with his lazy grin. That was Luc—laid-back, comfortable in his skin and always in a good mood. When she arched an eyebrow at him he simply shrugged. Obviously he was waiting for her to continue the investigation.

"What's your last name, Henry?" she asked.

"Brown. Henry Brown." His little chest puffed out. "I'm five and three quarters."

Five and three quarters. He was almost the same age as her baby...Holly gulped at the memories of that tiny innocent child and instead concentrated on what Henry was saying.

"Last night I stayed with this lady—Ms. Hilda." Henry's big brown eyes narrowed. His lips pressed together as he scrunched up his nose so his glasses would move back in place. "She snores."

"I see." Holly shot Luc a look meant to stifle his snort of laughter. She guessed Henry was one of the many foster kids from Calgary for whom Mayor Marsha often agreed to find temporary care.

Holly considered phoning the mayor but hesitated. Marsha was still recovering from complications after her second knee surgery. Maybe Abby Lebret, owner of Family Ties, would be a better choice. But it was barely 6:00 a.m. and if Abby's young twins hadn't yet woken her, she wouldn't appreciate an early-morning call, either.

"I want a family," Henry said with a glance over one shoulder, his voice and face as serious as a little old man.

"Me, too. Are you hungry, Henry?" Luc's grin flashed at Henry's emphatic nod. "Hey, me, too."

"Well, what's new about that?" Holly grumbled, irritated that her ranch manager didn't seem to be taking the situation seriously. "You're always hungry, Luc."

"Sounds like maybe you are, too, Miss Cranky," Luc teased, his eyes as warm as his smile. "Long shift, huh? What say we go get some breakfast?"

"Luc, you can't just take him—"

"Can I have pancakes? I love pancakes," Henry asked, his voice beseeching.

"Pancakes it is." Luc straightened. "We can come back here, Holly. When Family Ties is open," he added when she frowned.

"Well, all right," she agreed. "But we'd better phone Hilda first. She might be missing Henry."

"She's prob'ly still snoring." Henry's tone was utterly serious.

Holly had to turn away to hide her smile. When she did she bumped into Luc. He grasped her arms to steady her, which set her heart on a gallop.

"Whoa there, little lady. You must need some food if you're swaying on your feet." His hands dropped away but his gaze never left her face. "Did you forget to eat your lunch again?"

"I ate an apple around midnight," Holly said, avoiding his gaze. "I can take care of myself, Luc."

"Oh, I know that," he said, nodding, though his next words belied that. "But you do forget to eat when you're on night shift. Come on. Let's go to Brewsters." He swung his arm around Henry's shoulder. "They have the best breakfast," he said in a low voice.

"They have the *only* breakfast at this time of the morning," Holly corrected, noticing how easily Henry and Luc had bonded. Feeling left out, she dialed Hilda's. When there was no answer, she left a message on the machine then followed the two males while wondering how Luc knew she usually forgot her lunch.

He knew because he was always there for her.

Luc's being there had started the day he'd purchased the land adjoining her dad's Cool Springs Ranch. It continued after Holly's dad got a terminal diagnosis and elected not to fight his lung cancer. Marcus Janzen had chosen instead to live out his days at home. Since her mom had long since abandoned her daughter, husband and Cool Springs Ranch, Holly was the only one Marcus had left. Because she loved her dad dearly she'd focused her time and efforts on making his final days perfect, with Luc's help.

Marcus and Luc had become fast friends the day after Luc moved in to the neighboring spread three years ago. He'd shown up at Cool Springs that evening to ask Marcus about a sick steer. He'd come a hundred times since, eager to learn all he could about ranching from Holly's very knowledgeable dad.

Maybe that's why it had seemed normal for

Luc to "help out" as he put it, when Marcus fell ill. Luc did the chores her dad couldn't, sold the cattle Marcus wanted to part with and even sheared the sheep Marcus had just begun raising. After Marcus died, Luc kept coming back, kept helping out. And Holly had been glad of it, especially after Family Ties opened and, as the local nurse practitioner, she was called on to assist with several births.

"You must be daydreaming about something wonderful," Luc whispered in her ear when she passed through the door he held open. "Your smile couldn't get bigger. Something good happen?"

"Yes." She sank into a booth across from Henry. She smiled at him then faced Luc. "This morning I made a decision. I'm going ahead with the renovations on the house. I intend to make the extra bedroom into a full-blown sewing room."

She'd decided to go ahead because this morning the very thought of always having to clear off the dining table so she could sew the baby clothes she sold online seemed daunting. The extra bedroom was the perfect space; it just needed a few modifications.

Holly grimaced. Was it her good-girl image that made her try to gloss things over? Truthfully, that room needed a lot of modification if it was going to help her grow her business.

But Holly didn't tell Luc that. Nobody in town knew about her business and that's the way she intended to keep it. Getting dumped the day before her December wedding had generated enough gossip in Buffalo Gap to last a lifetime. She sure didn't need the town thinking she was so heartbroken and desperate to have a child that she now poured her soul into making baby clothes for other moms because she'd lost her chance to be a wife and mom.

"Holly?" Luc's touch on her arm roused her from her introspection. "Pancakes and sausage? That's what Henry and I are having."

"No, thank you." Holly made a face. "The very last things I want are heavy, syrup-drenched pancakes and sausages before I go to sleep. I'll have dry rye toast, two scrambled eggs and tea, please," she said to Paula Brewster. They shared a smile before Paula left to place the orders.

"Pancakes are good," Henry told her seriously. "Way better than eggs or cereal." He lost his serious look for a moment when Luc held out a hand to high-five him. But the gravity returned almost immediately. "When do I get my family?"

Holly didn't know how to answer. It would be nice to say "not long," to reassure the boy, but the truth was that neither she nor Luc knew anything about Henry and whether or not Family Ties could help him.

"That's a hard thing to answer, Henry," Luc said seriously. Holly liked the way he didn't brush off the boy's concern or make promises he couldn't keep.

"Why?" Henry's big brown eyes looked into Luc's trustingly, waiting for an answer.

"Because families are hard things to build," Luc told him. He grinned. "Look at me. I don't have a family yet."

"Don't you want one?" Henry thanked their server for his glass of milk, took a sip then leaned back in his chair to hear the answer.

"Definitely." Luc nodded. "But finding a family isn't easy. I grew up without my own family. Instead, other families took care of me."

"Did you like that?" Henry asked.

"Mostly I did. I was safe," Luc said after a moment of thought. "I had a place to sleep, good food to eat and nobody hurt me. It was okay."

"I want a family to love me." Henry's earnest tone matched his solemn face. "I prayed to God for it."

"That's the best thing you could do, Henry." Holly waited until Paula had served their food before she continued. "God loves us. He wants to give us what we most want. You just keep praying for a family."

"Do you have a family?" Henry studied her seriously.

"Not anymore," Holly explained quietly, setting down her fork as she spoke. "My dad died three months ago. He was all the family I had."

No way would she include her mother as family. Since the day she'd walked out, Holly barely gave the woman a thought and certainly not in terms of motherhood.

It struck Holly then that she'd done a much worse thing than her mother had done. The familiar burden of guilt that always accompanied thoughts of her baby settled on her spirit once more.

"I'm sorry." Henry reached across the table and enfolded her fingers in his. "I'll ask God to get you and Luc families, too."

"Thank you, Henry," Holly said, greatly humbled by his strong faith. "You'd better eat your pancakes while they're hot."

While Henry dug into his food, Luc bombarded her with questions about the changes she wanted to make to the farmhouse where she'd been born.

"Be more specific. What exactly do you want?" he pressed.

"I want more electrical outlets for one thing," Holly specified. "I want wide countertops to cut out fabric. I want better lighting so I can work at night if I'm on the day shift. I want lots of storage space and room for my quilting frame. If I get called in, I want to leave my sewing as is and pick up where I left off when I return."

"Shouldn't be hard." He shrugged.

"Good, because the dining table doesn't cut it anymore," she told him with a grimace. "I'm tired of making do."

"So am I," Luc said in a low-throated tone. "I'm really tired of that."

Holly stared at his serious face, confused by his words. But before she could ask him to explain, her phone rang. Mayor Marsha, who knew everything that happened in town, had already talked to Hilda about Henry. Pushing off her need for sleep, Holly agreed she and Luc would bring Henry to meet Marsha in the mayor's office in half an hour. Luc nodded when she told him then picked up their earlier conversation.

"I've never seen whatever it is you spend so much time sewing." He studied the green scrubs she still wore from her shift at the hospital, his gaze resting on the label on the chest pocket. "Not those, I'm guessing.

Are you helping with more quilts for Family Ties? I heard the intent was to give one to every woman who uses the services of Family Ties to adopt out her child."

"I am helping with that." Holly wished he wasn't so curious. "But that's not exactly what I want a sewing room for."

It was silly trying to evade the question because Luc never let anything go until he had an answer. That was the way he'd been the whole time he'd been learning ranching from her dad, and Holly doubted he'd ever change. His curiosity was innate. He was one of those people who asked and probed until he received a satisfactory answer. She thought Henry had the same trait.

"I could understand if you were still making your wedding dress." Luc squinted out the window, watching the town come to life. "But you don't need that anymore, do you?"

"Even if I did, it's too late," she told him defiantly. "I cut it up the day Ron dumped me."

"But you could use it someday," he protested.

"I am not getting married, Luc. Even if I were, do you honestly think I'd wear a wedding dress I chose to marry someone else? I assure you, I would not. But I repeat, I'm not getting married. Ever." She crossed her arms over her chest.

"Ever? That's pretty harsh." Luc raised an eyebrow then inclined his head toward her plate. At her nod he picked up the last slice of her toast and smeared jam over it. "Surely one day—"

"Never," Holly repeated. "I'm too independent." She glanced at him through her lashes as she fudged the truth. "I prefer to be single."

He shot her a look that questioned her statement.

"Don't worry. I put that wedding dress to good use. There are some really nice curtains in the living room at Family Ties." She burst out laughing at his startled look, hoping to hide the hurt that snuck up on her occasionally, ever since the day Ron had told her he wouldn't marry her.

That's what comes of keeping secrets.

"You're a good sport, Holly. I like that about you. Though I can't say I have such high regard for the man you chose to marry." Luc's voice tightened. "Ron Simard was a first-class jerk to walk away from you like that."

"He had his reasons." If Luc knew what she'd kept hidden from her fiancé until a few days before her wedding, Holly was pretty sure he'd have agreed wholeheartedly with Ron's decision to turn tail and run.

Luc had lost his family and frequently spoke of his desire for an heir. How could he ever understand her decision to give away the infant she'd birthed while she was in training?

"So your new sewing room doesn't have anything to do with Ron?" he pressed, nudging her from the past with its guilty secrets.

"Not at all! Sewing is my hobby, Luc, a way to be creative and a total change from my work," she explained. "It lets me achieve some of my dreams. Aside from the cost of the renovation, it shouldn't impact the ranch budget too much. Okay?" She stared at him, one eyebrow arched.

"If you're asking my permission, I certainly think it's okay if you make a sewing room out of your extra bedroom," he said, pushing away his empty plate.

"I wasn't asking your permission," she shot back, irritated that she'd felt compelled to explain but even more annoyed that she'd let him get to her. He knew it, too, judging by the smile flickering at the corner of his lips.

"If that's what you want. I might even offer to help you do the renovation."

"Really?" She frowned. "I thought you'd be too busy with ranch stuff. You keep asking if I've done it yet, but you've never actually offered to help me clean out Dad's trunk."

"That's different." Luc had the grace to look embarrassed. He turned, grabbed a napkin and wiped Henry's syrup-spattered cheeks. "I don't want to push in on your personal affairs," he muttered.

"Luc, you already know everything there is to know about Cool Springs Ranch," Holly pointed out, surprised by this sensitivity.

"There might be something personal in

there that you don't want to share. Did you ever empty it?" He did look at her then.

"Not yet." Holly couldn't shake the feeling that Luc was hiding something. "I'll get to the trunk. Eventually."

"Good. Anyway, renovating is different than going through personal stuff. Sort of." He nodded then shook his head. "Or maybe not."

"Definitive answer," she teased as she studied him, confused by his response. Luc was never uncertain. "You'll help me with the renovation and I suppose you'll expect me to help you with something in return. What?"

"I'm not sure yet." He tilted his head just the tiniest bit to the left where Henry sat silently watching them. Holly frowned, prepared to push for an answer but Luc shook his head.

She shrugged. Let him have his secret. Goodness knew she had her own and she hated it when anyone tried to push her into saying something she didn't want to.

"Can we get my family now?" Henry asked.

"It won't be that simple, Henry," Holly warned. "It's a long process to find a family. Besides, we've got another fifteen minutes before we're supposed to meet the mayor." His sad expression touched her. He must be very lonely. With a spurt of inspiration she asked, "Where did you live before, Henry?"

"In Calgary. In a shelter. My brother took care of me." For the first time the boy's composure fractured. A big tear plopped onto his cheek. "Finn can't take care of me anymore because he's in prison. He told me he didn't do it but I think he did steal the money from the store and it's my fault."

"How could it be your fault?" Luc asked, touching the boy's shoulder gently.

"My teacher said I need new glasses. But I shouldn't have told Finn because he didn't have any money to buy them." Henry's voice dropped to a whisper. "I asked him anyway."

"You couldn't know what Finn would do," Holly said, hugging Henry close for a moment. "It's not your fault."

When Luc didn't add his voice to the comment, Holly glanced up and found him staring at her and Henry, his brown eyes almost black with intensity.

"What?" she murmured, discomfited by his look.

"I just had an idea." A slow grin moved across Luc's face, accenting the handsome ruggedness. "Henry, here's some money. Could you go pay the bill?"

Delighted by this sign of trust, Henry scooted out of the booth and across the café.

"Why did you do that?" Holly liked that Luc was an open book. He didn't hide his thoughts or pretend to be anything but what he was—a cowboy. He was honest and straightforward and she knew she could count on him. So when he leaned toward her, Holly smiled, expecting a joke.

"In return for helping you with your renovations, I would like your help," Luc said.

"With what?" Surprised when he beckoned to her to move closer, Holly leaned toward him.

"With adopting Henry."

Luc winced when Holly's eyes widened then flickered with disbelief. What was so surprising about him wanting to adopt Henry? She studied him until Henry came back then turned her focus on the boy, watching as he first handed Luc the change and then began scribbling on his placemat with the pen he'd given him earlier.

"Henry," she said softly. "Mrs. Brewster has some toys over there, in the box under the window. Would you like to play with them for a few minutes until it's time to leave?"

"Okay." Henry shifted out of the booth, paused to study them through his big round glasses. "You and Luc should make a family."

"Uh, I don't think so." Holly avoided Luc's glance until Henry walked over to the toy box. "Where did he get that idea from?" Her beautiful blue eyes now had silver sparks in them which shot his way. "Never mind. Were you kidding about adopting him?"

"Why would I?" Irritated that Holly would

think he'd joke about such a serious subject, Luc clenched his hands on the leather bench. Why shouldn't he be a father to this needy boy?

Holly's glossy brunette curls, caught up in the ponytail she always wore to work, shone red-gold glints in a flash of sunlight coming through the window. She always looked lovely to him, but with the pink flush of annoyance now staining her cheeks, she was stunning. And she distracted him.

"You can't adopt Henry." Her voice had the sharpest tone he'd ever heard.

"Because?" Luc leaned back in his seat and waited, formulating arguments in his mind, ready to shoot hers down while wondering what was wrong with the usually happy Holly.

"You make it sound like it's a done deal, just because you've decided. Adoption's not that easy." Holly fiddled with her teacup.

"How do you know?" Funny how she didn't look at him now. Instead, she hid her gaze by staring at the uneaten food on her plate. Luc's radar was alerted, but he waited for her to speak.

"I've seen and heard stuff at Family Ties. There are procedures to go through. Isn't it time to leave?" Holly sounded almost desperate.

"We've still got several minutes," he said, wondering why she hadn't looked at her watch. It hung from a gold pin near her shoulder. Luc knew she did that because she'd once told him she disliked wearing anything on her wrist. He knew a lot about Holly. "What kind of procedures do I need to go through, Holly?"

"Uh, well…" She leaned back, obviously searching for an answer. "I don't know. Maybe start by learning all you can about adoptions. Check out support groups for adoptive parents or conferences where you can learn what to expect, what others have gone through, how to handle certain problems."

"Sounds like that would take a long time." There was something funny going on. Uncomplicated, straight-shooting Holly wouldn't look at him.

"Of course. Adoption is a long process," she said hurriedly. "You're adopting the child for life so it would be better to learn as much as you can before you act."

"I suppose." Luc nodded. "So what else do I need to know?"

"This isn't my specialty, Luc. I'm a nurse practitioner not a social worker." She sounded frustrated. Must be lack of sleep.

Luc knew ordinarily Holly would be tucked up in bed by now. She always gave her best at work but she worked doubly hard when she was on night shifts and especially when children fussed and seemed to need extra attention. Most mornings he watched her return home utterly worn-out.

"You're tired. Never mind," he said, sorry that he'd bothered her when she was spent.

"You should talk with Abby Lebret." Her voice sounded calmer. "She's the social worker who runs Family Ties and she'd know how to proceed."

"That's a good idea." He stretched out his

booted feet and bumped hers. "Sorry. I suppose someone will visit my place, make sure it's all right for a child to live there?"

"I'm sure that's part of a home study," Holly told him. "But I doubt you'll have just one meeting. It's—I mean I *think* it's more like a series of meetings and it gets pretty personal. Or so I've heard," she added, ignoring his surprised look.

"I'd expect to be investigated." Luc wondered where she got her information and then decided it must be from Family Ties. Abby and Holly were good friends. "I'd want them to get all their questions about me answered so there wouldn't be any mistakes that would mean they'd take Henry back."

"I guess that's wise. But, Luc, there's no guarantee Henry is even adoptable." Holly's smooth forehead pleated with her frown. "He might already be a candidate for some other family or it may be that he's not eligible for adoption."

"He is. I just know it." Luc couldn't explain how he knew Henry was supposed to be his son. He'd struggled for the past year trying to figure out God's will for him. Surely having Henry show up as he had, asking for a family, was a sign God's plan was for Luc to be a dad to Henry.

"I imagine Henry has a child worker assigned to him. I guess that person will be your first hurdle." Holly tried to hide a yawn behind her hand but didn't quite succeed. "I think we'd better get over to Marsha's office before I doze off."

"It's time." He waited while Holly collected Henry then walked to the door. "Are you going to stay awake through this?" he asked when she tried to smother another yawn.

"I can give you another half hour," Holly promised. "But then I am going to crash."

"Thanks, Holly. You have no idea how much this means to me." Luc reached out and squeezed her shoulder. With Holly on his side, he couldn't possibly fail to get his son.

Chapter Two

"Henry has no home. I don't see what's wrong with bringing him to my place to stay until the adoption goes through," Luc said as he took a seat at her dining table.

Holly watched as the tall, lean rancher gulped down a mouthful of the coffee she'd just poured, disregarding her warning that it was hot. Coughing and sputtering, he raced across the dining room to the kitchen sink and downed a glass of cold water. He made a series of silly faces as he tested his scorched mouth.

She tried but couldn't quite stifle her laughter at his antics.

"It's not nice for you to laugh at me, Holly," he reproved her then added, "Certainly not something the town's wonder girl would do."

"Oh, lay off that nonsense," she said, losing her good mood. "I'm not that wonderful and the town would know that if they really knew me." Sobered by his words she reminded him, "It's only been a week since you met Henry and you're still treating adoption just like that hot coffee. I warned you it was hot just as I warned you it wouldn't be easy to adopt Henry."

"I never thought it would be easy." Luc flopped back down in his chair and stretched out. "I just didn't think it would be a lesson in fighting bureaucracy."

"Please keep your boots away from that bag of fabric." Holly's warning came a second too late. "This is exactly why I need a sewing room," she complained in an exasperated tone as she freed a piece of frilly lace from the toe of his boot.

"Sorry. I know I promised I'd work on a sewing room in exchange for your help,

Holly. I'll get to it soon." He took the lace from her and studied it. "What is this for anyway? A hair bow?" He peered at it then studied her head. "Since when do you wear pink? You hate pink."

"It's not a hair bow and it's not for me," Holly told him, snatching the delicate lace from his fingers. "I'm going to sew it on a gift I'm making."

"*Another* baby gift?" He leaned over to study the fabric pieces lying on the table. "Looks like a jigsaw puzzle but I can tell it's for a girl. You sure do have a lot of new moms as friends."

"I deliver babies. It's my job to know the moms. I like to give them a little gift after their baby's birth." Holly flushed and looked away.

Shame on me for fudging the truth.

But how else could she explain without telling him about her online business? And Holly didn't want to do that. If Luc knew he'd probably pass on the information and soon the whole town would be talking. She couldn't bear to hear the gossips.

Poor jilted bride. That's why she makes baby clothes, you know. Because she doesn't have any children of her own.

If they only knew that she'd once held her own precious child in her arms and then given him away to save her father's reputation.

Since it was Holly's week off, Luc had made a habit of stopping by unexpectedly for coffee, ostensibly to discuss the work he did on her ranch. Somehow the conversation always turned to adopting Henry. A couple of times he'd caught her with her work spread all over the dining table. Well, it wasn't as if she could just scoop everything into a box whenever he appeared.

"I probably shouldn't have bothered you about this again," Luc apologized. "But I wondered if you'd given more thought to selling Cool Springs Ranch?"

"Not again." She rolled her eyes. "Luc, you've asked me that a hundred times since Dad died. I told you on Monday that I wasn't interested in selling any of Dad's land. Today is Thursday and I'm still not interested."

"It's not your dad's land anymore, Holly," Luc said in a somber tone. "It's yours."

"Yes, but he worked so hard to acquire this land and his herd," she said softly. "He wanted me to have a birthright." *Which should have gone to his grandson.* "I wouldn't feel right selling off any of it."

"Okay." Luc sighed. "But when you do decide, you'll give me first dibs, right?"

"If and when," she promised.

"Good enough." He wrinkled his nose at the brightly striped fabric she was about to cut. "That looks like clown material," he said then added, "Have you got time to go for a ride?"

"Now?" Holly paused, her scissors frozen in midair. She looked up at him and frowned. This was about the ranch; it had to be important. "What's wrong?"

"I'd rather show you than explain," he said. "Then I'll come back here and you can show me exactly what you want in your sewing room."

"Fine." Resigned, Holly put down her scissors and shut off the pattern mill in her brain.

If she had a bigger, more private work space, she'd be able to accept more orders and finally pay off the last of the bills leftover from her dad's illness. It was the only debt she owed him that she could repay. Nothing could ever make up for the love and care he'd showered on her all her life.

Except perhaps the grandson he'd never known.

"Holly?" Luc touched her shoulder. "Would you rather wait?"

"No. Let's go." She mentally shook off the past, knowing the guilt would return again later, when she was alone.

"It's the north quarter. We'll have to ride." Luc glanced at her bare feet and raised one eyebrow. "I think you're going to have to cover those," he jibed.

Holly glanced down and giggled.

"One of my Sunday school students gave me this polish," she said, wiggling her toes. "She said her mom thought it was too old for her."

"It's too something," Luc agreed, unable to stifle a laugh.

Holly laughed with him. Luc always had that effect on her, she thought as she pulled on her socks and riding boots. He was a very good friend who coaxed her to enjoy life. She enjoyed having him around.

They took the shortcut to the north pasture, past Luc's house. Holly slowed to a stop and squinted into the sun below the brim of her hat, waiting until he'd reined in beside her.

"What's that in your yard, Luc?"

"I'm restoring a truck and needed some parts so I had the garage tow in a couple of wrecks." He must have seen something in her face because he asked, "Why?"

"You're still determined to adopt Henry?" she asked, even though she knew he was.

"Of course. Why not?" Luc glanced at the yard then back at her. "What's wrong?"

"I think that whoever comes to check out your place will see those old cars and parts as a potential hazard for a kid Henry's age," she said gently. "You can still restore your vehicles but maybe not in front of the house."

"It's handy when I have a few minutes

after dinner," he explained. "I can walk out the door and work as long as the light's good, but you're right. I wouldn't want Henry poking around where there's a lot of rust and jagged edges."

"I'm sorry," she murmured, knowing how much he loved to restore vehicles.

"Don't be." Luc twisted to look at her, his grin back in place. "That's exactly the kind of thing I want your help with, Holly."

"Did you talk to Abby yet?" she asked. "She might have some weight with the government if Henry is in the care of Family Ties. Or even if he's under other stewardship."

"Abby told me Henry's only been in foster care since his brother went to prison, but that he hasn't been able to settle in anywhere. Apparently he doesn't like foster care and keeps asking for a forever family." Luc chuckled. "His case worker in Calgary was relieved Abby agreed to temporarily oversee his care while he's staying with Hilda Vermeer."

"He's still there, even though she snores?" Holly asked, tongue in cheek.

"Apparently there is a lack of foster homes right now. When he argued about staying with Hilda, Abby said she had to be very forceful with him to get him to understand that he'd never get his family if he didn't give her time to find it. Henry then said he'd wait a little longer." Luc laughed. "He's such a solemn, determined kid."

And you already love him, Holly thought, her heart pinching at the trouble that might lie ahead for Luc. And yet, she had only to think of the joy he'd experience as a father, joy she'd missed out on, joy she'd denied her dad.

"Henry reminds me of you sometimes," she said, not realizing she'd voiced her thoughts until Luc's eyebrows arched.

"Me? How?"

"His purpose, the way he won't give in, his certainty about what he wants from life. And his eyes. Henry's eyes are exactly like yours. Are you sure you weren't married and had a child you didn't tell anyone about?" Holly teased.

Luc's face tightened. "Never married," he

said firmly. "Never will. Some people, like you for instance, should be married. Some, especially if they're like me, shouldn't."

"Why not?" Surprised by the comment, Holly rode closer and tapped him on the arm. "Luc?"

He remained silent for so long she thought he wouldn't answer. She'd thought Luc simple and carefree until now. Her questions about him multiplied.

"I always intended to get married." He pulled his horse up when they came to the stream that divided their properties and dismounted. "That had been my dream since I was a kid, to someday have a wife and a family. A home. I thought with them I'd be able to make up for the family that I'd lost when my parents died in the car accident."

"And now you can't?" Holly's heart ached for the little boy he'd been and the grief he'd had to go through after losing the only family he'd ever known.

"I think maybe with Henry I can have that dream," Luc murmured thoughtfully.

Holly appreciated the way Luc held her

horse's harness so she could dismount, even though she'd been riding since she was five. There was something nice about having Luc do those polite things that made her feel cherished, special.

She sat down on a rock by the creek bed and waited while Luc fastened both horses to a tall poplar tree. He pulled two cans of soda from his saddlebags and a sack of nuts.

"I thought it'd be nice to take a break here," he said after handing her a soda. He folded his long lean length next to her then set his Stetson on a rock. His short dark curly hair glistened in the sun.

Luc, Holly suddenly realized, was a very handsome man.

"I love this spot. It's so peaceful." His voice rumbled quietly through the little glade. "It makes me think of God."

Holly sipped her drink and waited for him to continue. She, too, loved this spot and often came here to pray for forgiveness.

"This year I let go of the marriage part of my dreams," Luc told her, his face inexpressibly sad.

"Because?" Holly could hardly contain her curiosity.

"Because it wasn't realistic." A self-mocking smile stretched his mouth. "I thought love and marriage meant forever."

"And they don't?" Holly wanted to hug him when he shook his head. His face reflected his disenchantment.

"A month ago the woman I'd just proposed to told me she didn't love me enough to leave Calgary and move out here—to the back of beyond I believe she called it." Luc said it coolly, without emotion, but Holly saw the sting of rejection in his eyes.

"Oh, Luc. I'm so sorry." Holly frowned. "You never told us you were engaged."

"You and your dad had enough to deal with. Your canceled wedding and his illness took up every spare moment." His gaze rested on her, brimming with compassion. "My problems didn't matter."

"Of course they did. If you'd told us, we would have celebrated your happiness, even thrown a party." Holly pinched her lips. Luc grinned.

"Yeah, probably not a good idea," he said. "Too much to explain when we split up."

Holly couldn't suppress an oddly disquieting sensation at the knowledge that Luc had been contemplating marriage. She looked at him now with new eyes. Luc as a husband?

"Surely one breakup is no reason to give up on love and marriage," she said.

"It wasn't just one woman," he admitted in a low voice. "But this one hurt the most. Being rejected like that takes the starch out of you. It takes a while to get your feet back under you."

"Tell me about it," she muttered drily.

She wondered why she hadn't known he was in love. Then again, why wouldn't he be? Luc was very handsome, kind and generous, with faultless manners. Any woman would be fortunate to be loved by him. "I've been having second thoughts about marriage for a while," he volunteered.

"Why?" Holly hoped he wouldn't tell her to mind her own business.

"Several years ago I stood up at the weddings of several best buddies, guys with hearts of gold who'd gladly give you the shirt off their backs." Luc fiddled with his soda can. "I'd never seen them as committed as when they married their wives. They were determined to make it work, ready to put their all into it. Later they all had kids and seemed so happy. I envied them."

Holly said nothing, giving Luc time to gather his thoughts.

"I didn't know those marriages weren't even close to perfect. Now, one by one, each is ending in divorce." Luc swallowed. "The morning we found Henry I'd just come from my friend Pete's. He's the latest casualty." His face was troubled.

"Talk to me, Luc." Holly heard a world of pain in his stark words. He needed a friend and for once she *wanted* to be the one to help him.

"When I saw him, Pete was devastated, sitting in his truck, a shell of himself. He's lost his wife, his kids, his home. The love I envied five years ago is gone." He shook his head. "It was the most heartbreaking thing I've ever seen."

"I'm so sorry." The depth of his dejection touched her. "But that doesn't mean your relationships will fail. You just haven't found the right woman yet."

"I don't think love has to do with finding the right person, Holly. I'm not even sure there is a right person for me to find." Luc looked at her, his eyes dark. "Love is something you give, freely, unreservedly. How do you put your world together when the person you loved no longer wants you?"

"I wish I had the answer." Holly prayed desperately for words to soothe his stark hurt but couldn't find them. How could she help her friend?

"I'm no expert." His forehead pleated in a frown. "By everything I saw, those marriages should have worked. But my friends lost love and their dreams."

Holly felt stunned by Luc's desolation. She wanted him to expel the rejection from his heart so it couldn't hurt him anymore. As if! In five months she hadn't expelled Ron's accusations. Not yet. Not completely. "Go on, Luc."

"Sarah told me she didn't want to marry me after we'd been seriously discussing our future for several months." He shook his head as if he still couldn't believe it. "We'd even decided to get married in Tahiti because she said Buffalo Gap was too 'primitive.'"

That should have been a warning sign, Holly thought, but she kept silent.

"I agreed to almost all the conditions she set until she wanted me to sell my ranch." Luc smiled grimly when Holly reared back. "She told me she could never move here, so far from the city and her friends." Luc's face bore a pained look as if it hurt to admit the rest.

"I get the picture," Holly muttered, wishing she'd met this woman so she could have told her what a great guy Luc was.

"I didn't. Not until I insisted on keeping the ranch." His lips pinched together.

"Oh, Luc." Holly could almost guess the rest.

"She called Buffalo Gap Hicksville and hinted nothing here could possibly live up to city life. She said she wanted a husband to be proud of. She made fun of me for loving ranching, said I was wasting myself on cattle." His face telegraphed his sense of betrayal. "She said she wanted a husband to be proud of, not some guy smelling of manure, stuck in a mindless routine of chores."

"It's a good thing she broke it off," Holly burst out angrily. "Because if she hadn't, you would have. She would never have worked as a ranch wife."

"No, she wouldn't." Luc nodded. "But that's when I understood that I was just like my buddies. I gave everything to Sarah and she threw it in my face. That's when I knew that whatever I'd felt for her wouldn't survive the test of marriage. She hated everything I stood for. I made a mistake loving her."

"I'm not sure loving someone is ever a mistake. Love's not the problem," Holly mused.

"No, judgment is," Luc said. "My heart blinded me, which is bad enough. But my poor judgment is what scares me."

The sting of his admission reached deep inside Holly. Luc was one of the best men she knew. She didn't want him to hurt like this.

"I'm sorry," she whispered, knowing it wasn't enough.

"Now I know how you must have felt when Ron walked away, Holly. It's like being a kid again and having my world torn apart." His hands fisted at his sides and pressed against his worn denim jeans. "I will never go through that again."

"You can find someone else. There's nothing saying your marriage has to end like your friends' marriages did." Holly wished she knew how to help him.

"There's no guarantee it wouldn't. Sarah fit all my requirements for an ideal wife. That's why I started dating her. But I saw the outward beauty and missed what was inside. If we'd married and then split, it could have cost me the ranch..." His voice trailed away.

Love had cost Holly a great deal. She had no advice to erase the wistful sadness on Luc's face.

"I've accepted that I'm never getting married so it's a moot point now. But I refuse to give up all my dreams," he said sternly.

"I am going to have a son. That son will be Henry."

"Luc, I—" Holly stopped when his fingertips covered her lips.

"Don't say it, okay?" he begged, his voice soft, intense. "I need this dream so badly."

Holly frowned, wanting to understand.

"You don't know what it's like to suddenly lose your home, your family, everything. You're a little kid that no one cares about." Luc's intensity grabbed her heart. "I made do, I pretended, I fit in as best I could and concentrated on getting through."

Holly could see him in her mind's eye, a little boy, like Henry, pretending all was well, not making a fuss in case the family he was with asked to have him removed. And then at night, after the lights went out and he was alone in his bed, she could see him tear up, yearning for someone to say *I love you, Luc. I'm here for you. I'll always be here for you.*

That was the legacy her father had given Holly after her mother had left without saying goodbye. Pain stabbed her heart that Luc had lost that security. How could he not want to adopt Henry as his son and begin building his family?

"Dreaming of having a child was the one thing that kept me going through five very rough years in the oil fields." His face tightened. "I did some things, accepted some dangerous jobs on the rigs so that I could earn enough money to buy my ranch. I want to make a legacy, to reinstate the Cramer name as something to be proud of. I want to pass something on to Henry. He is the son I've longed for. I can't let go of this dream, Holly."

As his hand slid away from her face, Holly blinked at the loss rushing through her. She was heart-sore for this kind, generous man who only wanted simple things—a family, a home. Things other people took for granted.

"Then if that's your dream we'd better make sure there's no reason to deny appointing you as Henry's guardian, hadn't we?" she said finally. Her heart thudded at the joy exploding across his face.

"Thank you, Holly." Luc's smile made Holly's breath catch.

Why did she suddenly have such a strong reaction to him? Because she'd seen past the carefree persona he presented, to the man inside.

Luc was her best friend. Neither of them was willing to trust enough to love again. What they had in common only heightened their friendship. It was good to know nothing between them had changed.

And yet somehow it had. Holly now understood what drove Luc, comprehended his intense desire to make his ranch into a home, to adopt Henry. Luc would never walk away from that relationship. Somehow Holly knew he was trustworthy as surely as she knew her own name. Luc was a man of honor. In her life Holly had only ever known one man whom she'd found truly honorable and that was her dad. But Luc came in a close second.

Suddenly, unbelievably, Holly rejoiced that Luc had not married Sarah. She didn't deserve him.

You can't get close to this man, her brain

warned. *Not unless you're willing to share your secret with him.*

That inner voice unsettled her. "I guess we'd better go see what's bugging you up north," she said, needing to do something to escape her thoughts.

"Okay, but I'm warning you," Luc said as he rose and held out a hand to her. "Next time we come back here, I'm getting in that water." He nodded to the creek. "And I'm bringing Henry one day, too. Next to raspberry pie, swimming is my favorite thing."

He drew her upward too fast. Unprepared, Holly bumped her head on his chin. Good thing. She needed to snap back to reality because for a moment she'd seen herself in the picture, splashing Luc and Henry in the creek, as if she belonged there.

"I don't think I've ever known anyone who cooks like you." Luc held up one macaroni, bloated and tinged pink. "Who taught you to cook the tomatoes *with* the pasta?"

"Dad." She smiled at him, her sun-tinted face uplifted. "Don't criticize until you taste."

"Right." Luc popped the pasta into his mouth then held up his hands. "I stand in awe of you, Holly. You manage to make everything taste great."

"For your information I draw the line at cooking liver. I don't care how good they say it is for you." She giggled at his gagging motions. "I see we agree on that."

Luc nodded. "We agree on a lot of things."

"Like what?" she asked.

"We both like to eat." He snatched a radish from the salad.

Holly swatted his hand away but truthfully he thought she'd enjoyed the camaraderie they shared today. Luc wasn't sure he should have dumped his sad story all over her, but he needed her help with Henry and to get that, he'd felt compelled to explain his reasons for wanting to circumvent marriage. Maybe he'd let her see a little too far into his heart but he knew he could trust her. Holly was like a soul mate.

"So what will we do about those missing cattle and the ruined fences you showed me?" she asked after she'd said grace.

"I'll go up into the hills tomorrow and find those cows if it takes all day. But I need to figure out something to take the place of those fences where that steer was injured." He took a large helping of the macaroni and two pork chops, his stomach rumbling as he inhaled the delicious aromas.

"I guess it's been ages since Dad installed that fence."

Holly showed surprise when he told her the date he'd found in her dad's ranch note-books. "That long?"

"Yes. They've been repaired once too often. We need something else. There are coyotes in those hills and our cattle are too valuable to serve as their food." He paused. "Unfortunately, building a more solid fence means I'll have to cut down some of those gigantic spruce you planted with your dad."

Holly rose to get the teapot. When she returned to the table a tear glittered on the end of her lashes. Luc knew she was re-membering happy times she'd shared with Marcus, and missing him. How he hated causing her pain.

"Don't worry, I'll fix it, Holly."

"You always do, Luc. Thank you." Her gaze locked with his and in that instant he wondered if he should have embraced her. That's what Marcus would have done, and Luc had promised him he'd make sure Holly was taken care of. "You're a good friend."

Friend. His heart sank a little. Was that all he was? Some kind of long-distance acquaintance who never made it into the family circle? Luc chided himself. Holly and Marcus Janzen had always made him feel a valued part of their lives. From the moment he'd stepped onto their Cool Springs Ranch, Luc had felt at home. What more did he want?

More.

"What's that funny face about? Does my cooking taste that bad?" Holly asked in a worried tone.

"It's delicious," he reassured her. "I thought your dad was a good gardener but you're even better. Lettuce, onions, radishes—that's good for early June."

"I'm not just the town superstar you know," Holly teased with a self-mocking grin.

"Apparently not. What else have you got planted?" As far as Luc was concerned, Holly was as pretty as cotton candy, inside and out. He figured any man should be more than happy to forgive her for anything. Her fiancé obviously hadn't seen it that way. Again Luc wondered what had gone wrong between them.

Holly talked about gardening for a while. As she did, Luc studied her. She'd changed from her jeans and shirt into a pretty blue sundress that brought out her eyes. Her orange-tipped toes were bare again in a pair of comfortable-looking sandals. Her hair wobbled in a topknot that he expected to tumble down over her shoulders any second. She looked like the perfect rancher's wife. For somebody.

Though Luc could envision Holly as a wife, he couldn't settle on which of the available local guys would be the best candidate for her husband. Any of them would be lucky.

"You deliver a lot of babies," he blurted. "Have you ever thought about having your own?"

Holly's hand paused halfway to her lips. Her head went back and she gaped at him as if he'd asked where she'd buried her secret treasure.

"I didn't mean to offend you," he apologized. Why hadn't he kept his mouth shut? "I just thought that you'd naturally dream about your own kids and—"

"I'll never marry, Luc. I told you that." Her voice sounded hoarse as she set her fork back on her plate.

"You don't have to marry to have—"

"I'll never have children," Holly cut him off for the second time, exhaled and forced a smile. "I'm one of those women who don't have the motherhood gene."

"Not true." Luc speared a noodle and held it up for examination. Something was wrong. "I've seen you with your Sunday school class. Pretty sure you're what they call a born mother."

Holly said nothing. A moment later she

jumped up from the table and began making tea.

"I'm sorry. I guess your mom probably turned you off motherhood, huh?" he guessed, coming up with a reason for her jumpy behavior.

"My mother?" She turned to frown at him. "She never stuck around long enough to make much of an impact on me. It was Dad who was most hurt by her leaving."

"Really?" Unsure whether or not to continue, Luc pressed on, curious about her response. She was hiding something or else he didn't know this woman at all. "You were what—seven?"

"Almost eight. So what?" Holly returned to the table, completely forgetting the tea. She leaned her elbows on the table and crossed her arms as if to put a barrier between them. "She wasn't around here much even when she was supposed to be. Dad was the one who met me when I got off the school bus. As I said she didn't have an impact on me."

"Holly, it's okay to admit it." Why was she

so adamant? "I imagine all kids would miss their mother if she suddenly wasn't there."

"Well, I didn't miss her. Her absence never mattered because I had Dad. I always knew I could count on him." Her shrug signaled the end of that topic. "I drew a rough sketch of what I want in my sewing room. I'll show you after dessert."

"Dessert? Why didn't you tell me? I wouldn't have eaten so much." Luc let it go for now, but was determined to find out what kept Holly from admitting she missed her mother.

"I think it's very doable," Luc said after examining the bedroom she wanted renovated. "The costliest stuff will be the cabinets and countertops you put in."

He'd barely stopped speaking when Holly's cell phone rang.

"Hey, Abby. It's late for you to still be at work." Holly waited for her friend to explain. "He what?" She glanced at Luc and frowned. "Yes, I'll go look right now and I'll get Luc to help, too. I'll call if we find anything."

"Look for what?" Luc asked when she'd hung up, following her into the kitchen.

"For whom and it's Henry," she said as she kicked off her sandals and pulled on her boots. "He left Hilda a note."

"A note? Can Henry write?"

"It's kind of a picture note. Did you invite him to come to your place?" Her heart sank at his nod. "Well, apparently he decided to do that this afternoon, against Hilda's specific instructions. Some kids on their bikes saw him heading out of town earlier. He never came home for dinner. Hilda's frantic." She grabbed her jacket. "I'll saddle up Melody and ride her cross-country."

"Why cross-country?" Luc asked in confusion.

"Because the kids I mentioned told Henry the shortest way to your place was through Parker's Meadow." Holly watched Luc's face blanch. "What?"

"I put Ornery Joe in there yesterday," he said very softly. "That bull is mean. If Henry goes near him…" His words died away. They both knew the little boy didn't have a chance if the bull decided to charge.

"Let's go," Holly said.

"It wasn't an outright invitation to Henry," Luc said as he followed her outside. "It was just an offhand invitation like, 'You'll have to come see me.'"

"He's a little kid, Luc. He takes everything literally." He looked so upset Holly touched his shoulder. "Pray. Hard."

"I need to do more than that." Luc's face was tight with strain. He slapped his Stetson on his head. "How can I help?"

"Take my vehicle and go by road. Your truck can't handle the deep ruts as well as mine can," she explained, forestalling any argument. It was funny how they seemed able to anticipate each other. "Maybe Henry stuck to the road and didn't go for the short-cut. I hope. And, Luc?"

He'd been walking toward her jeep but now he stopped and turned, a question on his face.

"If you find him, you call 911 immediately

so they can call off the search teams. Not me, not Abby but 911. Okay?"

Luc nodded, a perplexed look on his face. "Of course."

"Good. Pray hard, Luc." Holly didn't take the time to explain. Instead, she raced across the yard to the barn where she saddled Melody and galloped across the fields, scouring wooded nooks and crannies for a little boy in a red-hooded sweatshirt who just wanted a family.

"Henry is Luc's dream," Holly prayed as she rode. "Luc's a good man. He's trying hard to be Your child." The reminder of Abby's words this afternoon sent a frisson of fear up her spine.

The case worker from Calgary is suggesting that Luc coaxed Henry out to his ranch after Hilda insisted they both wait for the visit till the weekend.

"Luc wouldn't do that. He's a wonderful man. He'd make a great father for any child," she whispered. "Please keep Henry safe and work this out so Luc won't be blamed. He was only trying to help Henry."

Holly spurred Melody to go faster. She had to find Henry; she had to make sure Luc didn't suffer for his eagerness to have the little boy in his life. As the wind dragged through her hair, Holly took shortcuts she hadn't used since she was a girl. Luc's words, filled with pathos, rolled through her mind.

Sarah said she wanted a husband to be proud of.

Silly woman. As if Luc wasn't that man! Fury spurred Holly on but she couldn't escape the echoed intensity of his words.

Henry is the son I've longed for. I can't let go of this dream, Holly. I just can't.

In that moment Holly decided she'd do whatever it took to help Luc realize his dream. She would never have another child, but Luc *was* going to adopt Henry if she had anything to do with it.

Chapter Three

He'd left his phone at Holly's!

Heart in his throat, Luc climbed the fence and moved forward while speaking constantly to Ornery Joe. From the corner of his eye he saw Holly arrive, slide off her horse and creep from tree to bush, edging ever nearer Henry who sat crying atop a big stone, the bull directly in front of him.

"Come on, you miserable grouch. Move over here. Leave the boy alone." Ornery Joe cast him a disparaging look, dug in one hoof and snorted before his gaze returned to rivet on Henry. For the first time since he'd become a Christian, Luc clung desperately to his faith. "God, we need Your help here."

Every so often the wind tossed Holly's words to him.

"You stay there, Henry. Don't get down. Don't even move," she said in a calm, even voice. "Luc and I will get you out of here but you have to stay still."

"I don't want to stay here," the boy sniffed. "I don't like that old cow."

"That's not a cow." Luc could hear amusement thread Holly's tone. "That's a bull. It's a boy cow."

"I still don't like him." At least Henry's voice had lost some of its sheer terror.

"He doesn't like you much, either," Holly told him. "Or me," she added when Ornery Joe lurched to his feet and lumbered around Henry's stone to take after her. Fleet-footed Holly scooted across some open ground and climbed a tree. "He sure doesn't like me at all. Get out of here, you grumpy old man," she yelled to the bull.

Luc had found nothing in Holly's jeep with which to entice the bull, except for a half-eaten package of chips. He rattled the foil bag now to draw Ornery Joe's attention.

"Here, boy," he called. "Here's a treat for you." He scattered the chips on the ground then looked toward Holly. "When he comes toward me, take Henry and run."

"What about you?" she called, her gaze intent on Ornery Joe who was watching them, swinging his big head from side to side.

"I'll be fine. You take care of Henry." Luc crackled the bag again then held it up, hoping the breeze would carry the smell of the chips to the animal. Sure enough, Ornery Joe lifted his head, sniffed then began to walk toward him. "Go," he said to Holly, hoping she'd hear him since he kept his voice low to avoid distracting the bull. "Go now."

In a flash she'd jumped down from her perch, picked up Henry and raced across the pasture to the gate.

Seconds later, certain she and Henry were safe on the other side, Luc backed up as Joe advanced. When the animal lost interest in the chips and glared at him, he turned and bolted, vaulting to freedom before Ornery Joe could get up enough speed to charge.

"You okay?" Holly called.

He nodded. "Just another pair of torn pants," he told her. "I caught them on a nail when I went over the fence."

"I'll mend them." Holly dialed 911 and said she was bringing Henry to town. Then she made another call. "We found him, Abby. He's fine. We'll meet you at Hilda's." Seconds later she slid her phone in her pocket before hunkering down to stare at Henry. "I'm mad at you," she said sternly.

Henry's eyes widened.

"Since when do you disobey the lady who's taking care of you? Poor Hilda's worried sick," she scolded. "That's rude and also wrong when she specifically told you she'd bring you to visit Luc on the weekend."

"I didn't want to wait," he said with a pouty look.

Interested to see how Holly handled this, Luc remained still and listened.

"Do you think Luc wanted to wait to have you for a visit? He didn't but he knows you can't always have what you want when you want it." Holly studied Henry, her severe look not dissipating. "Sometimes you have to be patient, Henry. Otherwise you end up in a heap of trouble, like you just did. That bull is very dangerous. You could have been hurt and all because you couldn't wait."

"I'm sorry." Henry's lower lip trembled and he ducked his head.

"I hope so. Luc risked his life to get you out, do you know that? If Ornery Joe had been really angry, he could easily have charged Luc or me." Holly paused a moment to let her words sink in. "Ms. Hilda knows about Ornery Joe. I'm sure that's why she wanted you to wait until she could take you to Luc's."

"I didn't know that." Henry sounded the tiniest bit belligerent. That didn't faze Holly.

"Of course you didn't and you didn't ask, either, did you?" When Henry shook his head, Holly made a clicking noise. "That's the thing, Henry. We all know you want a family and we're trying to help you, but you have to trust us." Holly brushed the hank of hair off his forehead. "We can't always tell you every single thing that's happening. You need to believe we're doing our best for you and be patient. Okay?"

He nodded slowly. "Are you still mad at me, Holly?"

"A little. You scared the daylights out of me." She pulled him into her arms and hugged him tightly. "Don't do it again, okay?"

"Okay." Henry hugged her back, his face wreathed in smiles.

"I think you owe somebody a big thank-you," she whispered just loud enough for Luc to hear. Her blue eyes glistened as Henry walked to Luc.

"I'm sorry I got in trouble," he said. "Thank you for helping me." He thrust out his hand.

Luc did the same. He looked at Holly, struggling to suppress his grin.

"You're welcome," he said as he shook Henry's hand. Then he scooped the boy into his arms, relishing the feel of holding this wonderful child. "But what are we going to do about my torn pants?" He set Henry down and showed him the tear in the back of his jeans. "These were my best ones, too," he mourned.

"Holly can fix them," Henry said with a grin. "Holly's good at everything."

"Not him, too," Holly muttered. Luc smiled.

"You should ask her to sew your pants," Henry advised.

"I'll do that." Luc shot a sideways glance at Holly who was looking anywhere but at him. "Something wrong?"

"Melody. She must have gone home. Guess I'll have to hitch a ride. But first we're taking Henry to Ms. Hilda's as promised. Let's go."

Luc waited, wondering if Holly would prefer to drive her own vehicle, but she waved him to the driver's side.

"I'm still shaking so much I'd probably crash us. He doesn't seem any worse for wear, though." She nodded toward Henry, who'd climbed into the back of the vehicle.

"You looked unflappable." He held her door. As Holly passed him, he murmured, "You were wrong, you know."

"About what specifically?" Holly gazed at him, her expression curious.

"That you don't have the motherhood gene." He saw a look of fear flicker through her gaze before her chin lifted. "I think you're a born mother."

"You're wrong, Luc." She stepped past him and into the vehicle. "I'm not the kind of mother any child needs."

Luc climbed in on the driver's side and drove to town. But all the way there he wondered why Holly was so sure she wasn't the mother type. The way she'd reprimanded Henry, firmly but gently, ending it with a hug, easing his fear but imparting the lesson of patience, was pure mothering. Surely she could see that.

Was there something in Holly's past that made feel she wasn't motherly?

Luc really wanted to find out.

"Thank you for finding Henry," Abby said as Hilda ushered the little boy away for a late supper. "I'm sure my call took you away from something important."

"Nothing's more important than keeping Henry safe," Luc said.

Holly felt his scrutiny, his earlier words replaying in her mind. Why hadn't she just let his comment about motherhood go? She'd only made him more curious. She also knew Luc well enough to know that he wouldn't stop until he'd figured out what was behind her comment. Stupid to have said so much.

But she was so tired of pretending. People in Buffalo Gap thought she had it all, that she never blew it or regretted anything. They only saw the perfect girl she'd tried to be so as not to disappoint her father, as her mother had.

But they didn't see the real her. Nor did Luc. Holly knew she was far from the perfect mother candidate. Perfect mothers didn't give away their newborn babies to save themselves shame or embarrassment. They certainly didn't forget about them once they'd given away their children.

But then Holly realized that despite her best attempts, neither had she forgotten. With every birth she assisted, every delivery, every prenatal class she taught she wondered, *Did my baby look like this? Is my baby happy? Where is my baby?*

There wasn't and never could be an answer to those questions. That's the way she'd wanted it. No shame or recriminations that her father would have to live with. At least that's what she'd told herself when she'd given up her son for adoption.

"Holly?" Luc was looking at her oddly. So was Abby.

"Sorry. Just thinking about Melody. She's still loose. I need to get home." And away from Luc's piercing stare.

"I'm sure you do. I just wondered if Henry had said anything to you about going to visit Luc." The speaker was a woman named Shelly whom Abby had introduced as Henry's case worker from Calgary.

"He didn't, but we did talk about what kind of things happen on a ranch," she said. "Henry asked how things worked and since I've lived on the ranch my entire life, I explained as best I could."

"Was your friend Luc there at the time?" Shelly asked, her gaze narrowed.

"No. I'd taken Henry out for a soda one afternoon, with Hilda's permission," she added. "He never said anything about visiting Luc then but kids get lots of spur-of-the-moment ideas and often act on them. Luc didn't tell Henry to come on his own if that's what you're insinuating," she insisted, disgruntled by the case worker's suggestive attitude.

"You're defending him." A smug smile tilted Shelly's lips.

"I don't have to," Holly said, disliking her more with every word. "He hasn't done anything wrong." She turned to Abby. "I really do have to leave. I can't afford to lose my horse."

"Yes, you and Luc go ahead. And thank you for your help. I don't know how we'd have managed without you." Abby hugged her and Luc.

"You do realize the police were called out," Shelly said to Luc.

"But that's what you do when a child is missing, isn't it?" he asked, a confused look on his face. Holly wanted to hug him.

"Come on, Luc. I need a ride back to find Melody." Holly tugged on his arm, relieved when he finally followed her from the house. She got in the driver's seat without thinking, started the engine and turned onto the highway toward home.

"Can you slow down a bit?" Luc asked in a mild voice.

"That woman! She was intimating that it was your fault Henry took off."

"I know." He smiled. "It was nice of you to defend me, but I didn't coax him to come."

"Well, *I* know that but Shelly doesn't. She seemed a little too ready to put a black mark against you." Holly sniffed. "I've seen workers like her before. So suspicious."

"I suppose she has to be when she's protecting a child who has no one else to do it for him." Luc sounded unruffled. "It's important to know that the people to whom you give the care of a kid like Henry won't abuse that trust."

"I suppose." Holly leaned back in her seat and took a deep breath. Thinking about the past always unsettled her. But she could hardly tell Luc that.

"Can I ask you something, Holly?"

"I guess." She twisted to look at him. The last vestiges of daylight were almost gone, leaving only the vehicle's dashboard lights to highlight his reflection.

"Before your fiancé," he said hesitantly. "Was there someone special in your life?"

What could it hurt to tell him? It had happened long ago. It was in the past.

"I can't imagine what prompted that question," she said, giving him an arch look.

"Humor me." Luc kept watching her.

"When I was going through my medical training I met a resident. Troy." Holly exhaled. "I thought I was in love with him but I was wrong."

"How did you come to think you were wrong?" Luc said quietly. "Did he decide that or did you?"

"He did, okay?" Talking of that time, remembering the decisions she'd made and questioned ever since hurt. She wanted Luc to let it go. "He told me he had plans for his life and they didn't include me. Then he walked away. I never saw him again."

Holly didn't tell Luc that Troy's plans also hadn't included the baby she was carrying. That was her secret and she intended to keep it that way. Luc was her best friend but as she'd learned to her cost, keeping your friends meant you didn't share absolutely everything.

Especially to a man like Luc who was desperate to have a child.

"It's good to get rid of that ugly wall board," Holly said right after she'd tossed a sheet of the offending stuff into the back of Luc's truck.

"Wood paneling isn't your favorite?" He was glad to see the smile on her face. For the past three days, ever since the Henry incident, Holly had been introverted, obviously stewing about something yet she refused to share the burden with him.

"It's dark and depressing. I don't know why Dad ever chose it. Or maybe my mother did. That would explain a lot about what went wrong in their relationship." She made a face at him then walked back inside her house. "Want some lemonade? I made it fresh this morning."

Luc nodded. He'd enjoyed these past few days they'd spent working on her renovation. Holly was fun to be with, full of great ideas and eager to implement them. She also didn't fuss about things like broken fingernails and dust as Sarah had on the four occasions she'd visited his ranch.

Luc sat next to Holly on the deck outside, savoring his drink and the warm spring afternoon. "Can I ask you something?"

Immediately, her eyes darkened and her face got what he termed her worried look. "I guess."

"Why is there an umbrella in your garden?" He watched her shoulders sag in relief.

"To shelter my pumpkin plant, of course." Holly's grin teased him as did her wink.

"Okay. That certainly explains it." Luc knew she was waiting for him to ask. "Why does your pumpkin need sheltering?"

"I just transplanted it. I'm trying to make

sure it doesn't dry out before it gets estab-
lished or get broken in a strong wind so I
shelter it for part of each day until it's hardy."
Holly sounded like a worried mom.

"Must be an important pumpkin." Luc
watched the sparkle return to her eyes.

"It is. It's a gigantic variety. I'm hoping to
enter it in the fair in August and win." When
Holly was excited like this, Luc couldn't take
his eyes off her. "First prize is five hundred
dollars. I'm also entering a baby quilt. First
prize for that is another five hundred. That
would go a long way toward a new sewing
machine."

"Great minds think alike. I'm hoping to
win a prize with the old truck I'm restoring."
Luc grinned. "And if I could win another
five hundred for being best historic entry in
the parade this summer, I'd be able to fix up
the '55 Chevy I've got stored in my barn."

"So we're both out to win." Holly chinked
her glass against his. "Good luck to us."

"What is it about sewing that gets to you?"
Luc asked curiously.

"What is it about fixing old cars that gets to you?" She shrugged. "I pick up a piece of fabric and I see how it could be used. I have to make it. Now you know how weird I am."

"Not weird at all," Luc told her. "That's how I am with old vehicles. I think I got that from my dad. I don't remember him much but I remember he loved old cars. I think he lived every moment of his life, like you." He smiled at her blush. Holly always tried to deflect praise. "Is it tonight Henry's coming for your wiener roast?"

"Uh-huh. And Abby and her family and Hilda and whoever else shows up. I kind of left the invitation for a spring picnic open." She chuckled at his raised eyebrows. "Well, it's really hard to know where to stop. This is the kind of place where everyone drops in. At least they did when Dad was alive. I don't want that to end."

"I wonder if Henry's ever had a wiener roast," Luc mused aloud.

"You haven't talked to him since the Ornery Joe incident?"

Luc shook his head. "No."

"Why?" Holly asked with a frown. "Have you changed your mind about adopting him?"

"No way. I want to adopt Henry very much." Luc couldn't come up with the right way to say it so he blurted it out. "I felt like you thought I should stay away from him."

"What? No." Holly's eyes narrowed. "If you'd asked I'd have suggested you keep seeing Henry as much as you can. You need to build your relationship so that the two of you will grow comfortable with each other."

"But—" Luc shook his head. "That's not the impression you gave that night we found him with Ornery Joe."

"I was worried, Luc. I thought that Shelly was looking for a reason to give you a black mark and I think I was right. Abby confirmed privately that Shelly suggested to her that you coaxed Henry to visit you, thereby superseding the authority figure she'd chosen—Hilda. But I don't think you need to worry about Shelly anymore."

"Why not?" He loved the way her face

glowed when she was excited or trying to keep a secret. "What happened?"

"Abby told me today that Henry's case has been transferred from the Calgary social worker to Family Ties. Abby's the case worker now thanks to Mayor Marsha's daughter in Calgary who is credited with getting the case moved here."

"And that means?" he asked, one eyebrow raised.

"That you don't have to worry about Abby because she'll give you a fair shake."

"This town," he said in pretended disgust. "You have to be in on the rumor mill to find out anything." In truth he loved that aspect of small-town life. Well, most of the time.

"Yep. Sometimes being the town mascot is good," she joked.

"The good citizens of Buffalo Gap do not think of Holly Janzen as a mascot," Luc scoffed. "More like a goal every child should strive to attain."

"I hope nobody tries to be like me," she said, her voice harsh. She fell silent for a while, her thoughts on something he couldn't share. But after a few moments, she snapped out of her bad mood to smile at him. "Now you need to solidify your case. Abby won't go against you, but she will take into account the efforts you make to get to know Henry. She'll probably be the one to do your home study, though I don't think that will happen for a while."

"That's a relief. I'm not finished with the spare room yet."

"Redecorating is a good idea." She sipped her lemonade. "It'd be different if you were adopting a newborn, but with an older child, I think placement officers will like the idea that you're making a special place for him, that you're preparing your world for him to be part of it."

"I don't know where you get all this knowledge," he said, studying her. "The internet?"

"Um, yes." Holly seemed startled by his question. "And Abby." She paused for a moment. "You should ask her lots of questions. She loves to explain."

"I don't think I can ask Abby how I'm supposed to mesh with Henry." Luc had thought adoption would be straightforward, but he kept coming up against more and more uncertainties. He hadn't realized he'd have to prove himself capable of fatherhood in so many ways. "She'd expect me to know."

"So?" Holly's blue eyes widened. "What's the problem?"

"The problem is that I don't have a clue how to mesh with Henry," he said, feeling inept.

"Sure you do." She rose. "You talked about taking him swimming when it got warmer. Maybe he'd like to fish. Or learn how to ride. What did you like to do as a kid?"

"Marbles." He followed her into the house, almost bumping into her when she suddenly stopped and turned to look at him.

"Marbles?" One eyebrow arched and she gave him a look that said "stop teasing me."

"I played marbles all the time," Luc told her. "And usually won, though I don't have a trophy for every time I excelled, like some people." He grinned when she groaned.

"Stop it, will you?" Holly said, her voice cool. "I don't have that many trophies."

"Are you kidding me?" Luc snorted. "Lady, I just moved boxes of them from your spare room. Horsemanship, curling, baseball, friendship leader, junior citizen of the year, debate team, valedictorian, highest science test scores—to name a few." He stopped ticking them off his fingers and faked a sigh of exhaustion. "Is there anything you didn't win a trophy for?"

"Dealing with men who promised to renovate my spare room then ended up talking too much," she shot back pertly.

"Low blow." Luc clutched his chest and pretended to swoon.

"Can we get back to Henry? Maybe he'd like to learn to play marbles." Holly stored her drinking glass in the dishwasher with his and checked the clock. "I think we could get the rest of the paneling out before I have to start putting together dinner for my guests."

"How hard can it be to put together a few hot dogs?" Luc knew the minute he said it that it was the wrong thing to say. She glared at him then plunged her hammer right into the middle of a sheet of the despised paneling. "Um, I could help you with—whatever," he offered.

"I'd appreciate it, but let's finish this first. Then we'll see how much time we have left." Holly's no-nonsense tone told him she wasn't ready to forgive his comment.

Luc liked the way they worked together, each anticipating the other's moves. In no time the room was stripped, except for her father's big trunk in the corner. He looked from her to the trunk and back again, eyebrows raised in an unasked question.

"You have an obsession about that trunk." She scowled at him. "I'll sort it out."

"Just not today, right?" He shrugged. "Fair enough. How many more days off do you have?" he asked as they hauled out the last of the trash and threw it in his truck bed. He'd get rid of it later.

"Only two and that's if the hospital doesn't call me in." Holly sighed. "And then there's Family Ties. Abby phoned to tell me a new girl arrived yesterday. Seth Treple was called in to examine her and he feels she's close to her due date so I'm on call."

Seth was the local GP who'd agreed to handle Family Ties' patients, both mothers and children when Holly couldn't.

"Seth can't deliver the baby?" Concern tugged at Luc as he noted the weary lines around Holly's eyes. It didn't seem as if she was getting the rest she needed. "You've been covering for him a lot. I know that as a nurse practitioner you're more than qualified to do most things he does, but you've been logging a lot of hours lately. You deserve your days off."

"Babies don't fit a schedule. Besides, Seth needs a couple of days off to visit his sick mother in Calgary." She shrugged. "It's fine."

It wasn't fine that she was almost dead on her feet. Maybe this demolition was too much for her, on top of everything else in her life. But he noticed Holly admiring the empty area.

"Soon all this will be sewing workspace." She sounded enthusiastic.

"Hopefully." Luc checked his watch. "I'm guessing we have about an hour until your guests will arrive. What do you need to do to get ready?" There was no point in telling her to relax for a minute. Holly did what needed to be done. Tiredness wouldn't stop her but maybe he could ease her load.

"To get a few hot dogs ready?" She shot him a look. Apparently not prepared to let him live down his earlier comment. "I've got to haul the tables from the shed and set them around the lawn. Spread out some chairs. Build a fire. Assemble the snacks. Change clothes and set out the food and—"

"Okay, stop. I'll do the outside stuff. You change and get the food ready." He loved the way her smile spread across her lips right up to her lovely blue eyes.

"Really? You're sure you're not too tired?" She threw her arms around him and hugged him. "You're an answer to my prayers, Luc." One more hug and then she raced into the house.

Luc stood where he was, taken aback by her hugs, but even more astonished by how much he'd enjoyed them.

"Something wrong?" Holly called, her head stuck out the door.

"No. Just planning." He walked toward the shed, touching his cheek with his forefinger where her lips had rested if only for a nano-second. In all the time he'd known Holly, she'd never hugged him.

He'd only managed to set up one table when Abby and Cade Lebret arrived with their twins and Ivor, a foster boy they'd adopted. Cade and Ivor helped Luc lug out tables and chairs while Abby took the twins to the house. Ivor begged to start the fire so Cade hunkered down and showed him how to start one with shavings then tinder then sticks and logs. Luc stood watching, think-ing that soon he'd be able to do the same thing with Henry.

As others began to arrive in the yard, Holly emerged from the house. Luc caught his breath. Her skin glowed against the aqua-marine top she wore with slim black jeans. Her dark curls tumbled loosely over her shoulders. His heart raced like a steam en-gine when she smiled at him and thanked him for setting up.

"You've done a great job," she praised him.

"All that's left is to bring out the food. Would you mind helping with that, too, or would you rather visit?"

And miss another of her embraces?

"Lead on," was all Luc could say as he followed her inside the house.

"There's a ton of stuff." She pointed to a lime-green bin Luc figured weighed nearly fifty pounds. "Table coverings, cutlery, candles, et cetera in that one."

"Okay." He watched her pick up another bin. "Is that as heavy as this one? Somebody else could carry it."

"Hey, I'm no weakling." Her blazing smile did funny things to his pulse. "Don't worry. This one has paper plates and plastic glasses. It's light but thanks for your concern." She hurried out the door in front of him.

Luc followed, wondering why lately his knees went so rubbery whenever he was close to her. Once he'd set the box down, Holly took over, spreading plastic cloths and directing him as they loaded the table with everything they'd need. A few minutes later he noticed Hilda's car trailing dust as it headed toward Cool Springs Ranch.

"Okay, let's get the food." Holly hooked her arm through his and drew him toward the house. "Isn't it a perfect evening?" she enthused.

When they returned with food trays, Luc noted that Cade and some of the other men had cut roasting sticks for the wieners. The fire blazed. A moment later he heard Henry yell.

"Hi, Holly. Hi, Luc." Henry shoved his glasses up on his nose right before Holly threw open her arms and the boy rushed into them.

Holly giggled and laughed as she spun him around in a circle of joy. Then she set him down and said so quietly Luc almost missed it, "Luc's been waiting for you to arrive, Henry."

Henry seemed suddenly shy. He stood where he was, staring at Luc who grinned at him and stepped forward.

"Hey, Henry." The boy held out a hand to shake but Luc needed more than that. As he scooped Henry into his arms, he glanced up and found Holly watching, a wistful look on her face. It seemed as if she should be in the circle with them but suddenly she moved away.

Her voice emerged a little tight as she called everyone to join hands before Mayor Marsha said grace. Somehow Luc ended up with Henry on one side and Holly on the other, her hand clasped in his.

As if it belonged there.

But Luc was pretty sure that wasn't God's plan for his life.

Chapter Four

On a balmy June evening, Holly pulled up to her home on Cool Springs Ranch with a sigh of relief.

"Thanks for the safe trip, Lord," she said after she'd switched off her car. "Sometimes I forget You're with me all the time, even when I get stuck in past memories."

Determined that tonight she would not get dragged down to that place of guilt and regret from the past, she climbed out of her jeep then began unpacking the results of her shopping day.

"Can I help?"

Holly squealed in surprise and whirled around, bags flying.

"You scared me half to death, Luc," she told him with a groan. "What are you doing here so late?" She wrapped her arms around the parcels he handed her and smiled her thanks when he unloaded the rest from her vehicle.

"I had a few spare hours and I thought I'd get started on drywalling your room. You did say to come and work even if you weren't here," he reminded.

"I said it and I meant it." She started toward the house. "It's just that you mentioned branding the new calves today and I thought you'd be busy with that."

"Finished before noon." He grabbed the screen door and held it open for her.

"Thanks." Unable to corral her packages any longer, Holly let them drop on the dining room table. "You can put those here, too," she told Luc.

"I'm not sure they'll all fit. What did you do, buy out the store?" he joked then did a double take at the look on her face. In a hesitant tone, he said, "Holly?"

"I received a phone call last night from my

favorite fabric store in Calgary. They were holding a one-day sale today. Fifty per cent off everything." Her shoulders sagged as she sat down, slid off her shoes and flexed her toes. "So I went. And I bought. A lot."

"Is that all? I thought maybe something bad had happened."

"That *is* bad, Luc," she moaned. "I overspent. A lot."

"But you needed this fabric for whatever you're sewing, right?" He waited for her nod. "So you weren't wasteful or spending for spending's sake, right?" He waited for her nod. "So why should it bother you that you got a good deal?"

"I hope this doesn't come out the wrong way," she said finally, "but your Sarah was an idiot to let you go. I've never heard another man approve a woman's overspending on shopping."

"I am truly a man among men," he said with a grin.

"Now I've fed your huge ego." Holly shook her head then leaned down to rub her foot.

"All that shopping has given me an awful cramp in my foot."

"Neither you nor Sarah has any idea of just how wonderful I am." He preened. "I happen to know all about foot-itis."

Luc sounded as if he'd begun to shed some of his hurt over Sarah and she was glad. But when he snagged a chair leg with one foot then drew it near so he could sit in front of her, Holly stared. Then he lifted her foot onto his knee.

"Uh, what are you doing, Luc?" She wiggled her foot, trying to free it.

"Hold still and you'll find out," he ordered. When she'd settled he explained. "One of my foster moms used to get terrible leg cramps after a day of work. The first thing she taught me after I moved in was how to help her. Relax, Holly."

Holly wasn't sure she *could* relax with Luc's strong fingers pressing and kneading her sensitive foot. Every time he touched her it was like a spark shot through her. But after a few moments she had no doubt he knew what he was doing. She closed her eyes and let him work the kinks out of her toes. She'd almost drifted off when he gently set her feet on the floor.

"Better?" he asked quietly.

"Much," Holly breathed. She blinked her eyes open and smiled at him. "Give me your foster mother's name. I want to send her flowers. Maybe Sarah, too. Her loss is my gain."

Luc chuckled, his dark eyes bright with laughter. "I'd better put away my tools and get out of your hair. Then you can admire your purchases."

"Do you ever just go out and splurge, Luc?" Holly asked, unable to contain her curiosity.

"I splurged when I bought my ranch," he said thoughtfully. "I'll be paying for that for a while. I need to set aside money to raise Henry, too, so I can't afford too many splurges." He walked toward the spare room. "But if I did, the last thing I'd buy would be frilly fabric."

"Ha-ha. Did you eat supper?" Holly could tell from the look on his face that he hadn't, though he neither confirmed nor denied it.

"I have a steak thawing in the fridge. I'll share it with you in exchange for the foot rub. Deal?"

"Of course I accept." Luc's grin stretched across his face. "My foster mothers didn't raise a dummy."

She liked the way he was so at ease with his past. A lot of men wouldn't have been able to accept losing their parents let alone joke about being raised in foster homes. Luc was so comfortable with who he was but then he didn't have to live up to a whole town's expectations.

"Give me ten minutes then you can grill the steak on the barbecue," she promised.

"I'll finish up what I was doing." Luc disappeared into the bedroom. Seconds later the sound of a drill echoed through the house.

Holly scooped her purchases into her bedroom closet, changed into her favorite jeans and T-shirt and hurried back to the kitchen. When she'd finished baking the potatoes in the microwave, made a salad and fired up the grill, she went to find Luc.

"I can't believe you've made so much

progress." She surveyed his work from the doorway. "Except for that wall." She frowned at the unfinished studs.

"That's the wall where the new outlets will go," Luc explained. "I'm waiting for the electrician."

"Oh." The room looked huge. When it was finished she'd have tons of storage, a functional work area and a great view of the hills through the new window he'd installed. "I can't thank you enough for doing this, Luc."

"It's going to be a good work space," he said with a nod. "And I'm getting a great exchange with you helping me with Henry." His eyes twinkled. "I took him for a milkshake after school today as you suggested. With Hilda's permission," he added with a wink.

"How'd that go?" Holly's heart bumped when he flashed his amazing smile at her. He looked handsome and proud and thrilled.

"Great." Luc's smile grew. "Henry's got a slew of new knock-knock jokes for you."

"I can hardly wait." It was obvious he'd enjoyed every moment of his time with Henry.

Holly chided herself for feeling envious of the affection he lavished on the boy. She *wanted* Luc and Henry to bond, so where did that emotion come from? Not willing to search for an answer, she changed the subject. "Time to grill," she told him.

"My favorite way to cook."

Holly sat outside on a lawn chair, sipping a cup of the coffee she'd just brewed, while Luc barbecued. Before she'd always been at ease around him, like anyone would be with a good friend. But this evening that comfortable feeling eluded her. She felt the need to fill the silence gaping between them.

"When I stopped in town for gas on the way home I heard that James Cooper is looking for a partner to buy the old McCready homestead." She didn't understand his frown. "Buying it would be a way to enlarge your ranch, wouldn't it? The land adjoins yours."

Luc flipped the steak like an expert. But then he did most things competently. And he was so easy on the eyes that Holly kept watching him.

"James phoned and offered me a partnership but I turned him down," Luc said.

"Why? You're always going on about adding land to your spread." His refusal perplexed her.

"I want to buy Cool Springs Ranch." He turned to glance at her. "Not the McCready place."

"Again, why?"

"The McCready ranch is too rocky for one thing and the low parts are subject to spring flooding," he explained. "Besides, I want to own my land, not share it. I can wait for yours."

"But, Luc, I may not be ready to sell Cool Springs for a long time." Holly was aghast that he would put his plans on hold indefinitely. She felt guilty and somehow responsible for staying here and thereby denying him his dream.

"I know. I'll wait," he repeated. "Meantime I'll save my money, so when you do decide to sell I won't need a big mortgage."

Though he tossed her that warm, easy grin, Luc's words troubled Holly.

"But what if I never sell?" Luc couldn't just sit and wait for her to leave Cool Springs Ranch because Holly had no plans to do that. Despite the pressure the locals put on her, this was where her friends and neighbors were. This was *home*.

"You won't stay here forever, Holly," Luc said imperturbably.

"I won't?" She blinked, curious yet hesitant as to why he said that. The warmth in his dark gaze made her feel cherished, protected, as if Luc truly cared about her and her future.

"Holly, it's obvious despite your denials that you're meant to be a wife and a mom."

"I told you—"

Luc stopped her by simply raising his hand. He scanned her from the ribbon that held her hair tied at the top of her head, to the toes of her feet, now snuggled into comfy moccasins. That scrutiny made her skin tingle.

"You love babies and kids, Holly. That's why you chose the career you did. One day you'll meet some guy and fall in love with him." His voice was very quiet. "You'll get married, move to your husband's place and I'll buy Cool Springs from you."

"I've told you. I am not getting married. Ever." Irritated, she rose, tossed out her coffee into the flower bed and walked through the patio doors.

Two minutes later, Luc followed her with the steak sizzling on the platter she'd left by the barbecue.

"I wasn't trying to annoy you, Holly. I was just telling you what I believe." He set the platter on the table then studied her, his head tilted to one side. "Forgive me?"

"There's nothing to forgive." She wasn't going to discuss it anymore so she motioned him to sit down, brought the potatoes from the microwave and carried the salad over. "You want to say grace?"

"Sure." Luc closed his eyes and bowed his head. "Thank You, Lord, for this day and for Holly's good food. Bless her and me as we share this meal. Amen."

He was even comfortable saying grace, Holly mused. Funny that only now after he'd revealed his relationship with Sarah did she truly realize what a remarkable man Luc was—utterly kind and likeable. She cut a small piece of steak for herself and left the rest for him, puzzling over this increasing appreciation of him.

"You're spending a lot of time on my project," she said. "I hope it's not making you ignore other chores?"

"Are you asking me if your foreman—me—is shirking?" The corners of Luc's eyes creased with his amused grin. "Would I do that after learning how to ranch at your father's knee?"

"You think Dad didn't slack?" Holly chuckled. "Maybe you weren't paying close enough attention. Dad often rushed through his most demanding chores, sometimes left others undone so he could inspect his bee-hives."

"I never understood why bees fascinated him," Luc said thoughtfully.

"*Fascinated* is the word. He used to say they had secret lives and that only God knew what they did all day." Holly laughed out loud. "When I was little he'd tell me stories about a character named Benny Bee and how he was buzzy doing God's will."

"Buzzy?" Luc smiled. "Now I think of it, Marcus did use the word *buzz* a lot."

"Remember he used to tell you to buzz off when he got tired of answering your questions?" She giggled at his sheepish grin.

With Luc across the table, her plain fare tasted delicious. There was a lot to like about sharing a meal with a friend like him. Holly hadn't realized how much she'd missed sharing relaxed moments like these with her dad. She closed her eyes and let the memories swamp her. When Luc cleared his throat she smiled at him through her tears.

"I miss him."

"Me, too," Luc said. He reached out and squeezed her hand. "He loved you very much."

"I know." She swallowed the lump in her throat and changed the subject. "As I remember it, Dad also had a lot to say about God's will."

"That's a topic I wish I could quiz him on now." Replete, Luc leaned back in his chair.

"Oh?" Holly poured them each a cup of coffee as she waited for him to continue.

"I didn't just work on your room this afternoon," Luc admitted. "I spent about an hour on the phone with my buddy."

"Pete, the one whose marriage is breaking up?" she guessed, wincing at the sad look in Luc's eyes.

"Yes. He hasn't been a Christian for much longer than I have. He has a lot of questions about God's will that I can't answer." He looked at his hands as if he was embarrassed by his own ignorance. "Learning God's will is something I've also been struggling with. Got any ideas I could use and also share with him?"

"I'm not really good at giving spiritual advice," Holly said, feeling like that was the understatement of the year. Lately, guilt had almost convinced her she'd failed at being a Christian but she kept up her faith despite the way she'd botched her past. But now she couldn't ignore the pain in Luc's words. "I've heard lots of sermons about God's will. If you want to share what's bothering you I'll listen. Maybe I'll remember something that will help you."

"Thanks." Luc played with his fork for a few moments before he looked directly at her. "How do I figure out what God's will is for me, Holly?"

"You don't ask the easy stuff, do you?" She took her time arranging her thoughts. "I think it depends how you mean the question. If you're talking generally then God's will is for you to accept that His son died for you and live as His child."

"I'm trying to do that every day," he said with a nod. "But it's the specific details, what God intends for me personally in my future that I can't figure out."

"That is hard to know. I've questioned that, too. 'Does God want me to do this or this?' It would be nice if there was a bolt of lightning that pointed the way, wouldn't it?" She sighed. "But I've never seen God work that way."

"How do *you* understand His will?" His desperation reached into her heart.

Holly didn't like revealing details about

struggles in her faith journey. It seemed too personal, opened up a part of herself that she'd always kept hidden. And yet, Luc wanted her help. She couldn't brush him off. She whispered a prayer then inhaled.

"I start by studying the Bible," she began. "I believe that's where God has put the answers we seek. Of course it would be easier if He would thump us over the head with His will, but I think learning what He wants us to do is supposed to be a journey of discovery."

"Really?" Luc looked skeptical.

"Really. Think about it. My dad could tell me twenty times over how to saddle a horse, but until I figured it out for myself it wasn't meaningful." She grimaced. "Falling off because I'd forgotten to tighten the cinch personalized it in a way his words could never do."

"How could Holly the perfect rancher's daughter ever forget a thing like saddling a horse?" Luc chuckled, his dark eyes dancing with teasing.

"I never claimed I was perfect." His words

put a damper on her spirit. There were those expectations again.

"*Perfect* is what everyone in town calls you," Luc shot back.

"I know." She made a face. "I tried so hard as a kid to make up for my mother's leaving, to never have my dad be ashamed of me. Too hard, apparently." Luc's uplifted brows made her hurry to explain. "My dad was devastated by her departure. I saw that and thought he'd forget her and love me more if I achieved. I wanted to be a daughter he was proud of."

"Your dad would have been proud of you no matter what, Holly," Luc said softly.

"I didn't understand that. I thought I could heal his pain. I didn't understand till years later that nothing I did could take her place for him. Back then I kept pushing to be the best I could be." She swallowed hard, amazed that the memory of that confused, painful time still had the power to hurt. "It's my own fault nobody sees the real me," she murmured. "All they ever knew was the image I projected, still project I guess. Holly the overachiever."

Holly hated the gush of hurt that always swamped her when she admitted to herself that she lived a lie, that ultimately she'd failed to be the exemplary daughter she'd striven so hard to be. She was the local golden girl tarnished by a major mistake. She'd given away her child, let someone else raise the grandchild her father never knew because she hadn't wanted her dad to be ashamed of her. Worse, she hadn't wanted the town to realize how far she'd fallen from the pedestal on which they'd placed her. She'd never realized that what others thought would never make up for the loss that now plagued her.

That was why she couldn't open that trunk. She didn't want to hear her father's praise and know she wasn't worthy of it. She'd tried to accept that the only important opinion was God's, but she'd failed Him, too. It was a burden she couldn't break free of. How could God ever forgive or forget her sin?

Holly studied Luc's face, suddenly curious to know what he'd think of her if he knew the truth about her. Luc was all about children, a heritage, a legacy. Deep down inside she knew he'd never countenance giving away a child she should have loved and protected. His reaction would mirror Ron's. Luc would be disgusted by her willingness to abandon her principles to maintain a charade, to protect herself.

That's why she'd never tell him or anyone else in town about her baby.

"Holly?" He urged her from her reverie. "God's will?" he nudged.

"Sorry." She regrouped and continued. "If the answer I'm looking for isn't clear, I pray for a specific answer, like asking God to do something special so I'll know I'm in His will."

"But I've done that and I'm still unclear," he said with a frown.

"I'm sorry, Luc." She smiled, but her heart ached for his confusion. "Sometimes it's a matter of moving ahead with the information we have and trusting that He will guide us where we should go. Maybe that's where you are at," she suggested.

"But what if I misjudge what He's saying?" His eyes bored into hers with an intensity that made Holly shift uncomfortably.

"That's how we learn. We start over and try to do better." Saying those words made Holly feel like a hypocrite. How could she possibly start over from her mistake?

"You don't sound convinced," he teased. "But then given your dad and the home you had, I doubt you've ever made any serious mistakes."

"You'd be surprised." Exceedingly uncomfortable with the turn of the conversation, Holly rose and began clearing the table.

"I'm sorry." Luc's hand covered hers. When she turned to glance at him, his face was mere inches away. "That wasn't very sensitive. I'm sure you've had lots of struggles, Holly. I didn't mean to diminish them."

"I've struggled with being in God's will for years," she admitted quietly before moving away from his touch.

"Really? But you know your future. You have a great career. You're there whenever someone needs you." Luc paused. "What is there to question? You're *in* His will."

"If I am, then why didn't I know my fiancé wouldn't be able to accept—" She stopped before she blurted out her secret to Luc. He was too good a listener. "When I didn't know he wouldn't be able to accept what I told him? That was a humiliating mistake to make." She was utterly embarrassed to discuss this with him.

"At least you didn't marry the wrong guy." Luc touched her shoulder and turned her so he could look into her face. The sympathy she saw there soothed the stinging hurt inside her heart. "God saved you from making that mistake, Holly."

"I wish He'd chosen a less public way," she mumbled. "Everyone in town...and everyone at any wedding...they look at me with pity. I hate that."

"I doubt anyone pities you," Luc said. "If there is pity, it's for Ron. He has no idea what he missed out on by dumping you."

"That's nice of you to say." Holly turned

away to load the dishwasher, trying to hide her blush at the depth of sincerity in Luc's voice.

"It's the truth. Any man would be proud to have you for his wife, Holly. Don't let Ron turn you off marriage."

"It's not just that." She poured two fresh cups of coffee and set them on the table along with the tarts she'd bought that afternoon. She waited until Luc was seated, too. "You're talking about God's will."

"Yes." He waited patiently for her to organize her thoughts.

"I don't believe I'm supposed to be married." Before he could speak she hurried on. "That's not a reaction to my canceled wedding, it's *because* of it. I think God has something else in store for me, so that's why I'm confused about His will. I don't know what that something is."

Luc wasn't exactly sure why he hated hearing Holly reject marriage. In his mind's eye he could see a little girl with Holly's turned-up nose and bouncing curls running across the field after a baby lamb. The movie in his mind widened to include Holly, her bubbling laughter floating on the breeze as she chased after her daughter. She scooped up the little girl and hugged her close, whispering "I love you."

She was so meant to be a mom.

"Luc?"

He blinked back to reality. "Yeah?"

"Can I ask you something?" Holly waited for his nod. "When you talked about Sarah, you said you two broke up because she wouldn't move here."

He nodded, wondering where this was leading.

"In hindsight, do you think that if she had agreed your marriage would have been a success?" She stared at him, waiting for an answer he didn't have.

"I don't know." Looking at Holly, Luc realized he could barely recall Sarah's features. He only knew she'd never looked as pretty as Holly did now, the lamplight bathing her in its glow.

"I don't think it would have," she murmured, her face pensive as her gaze held his.

"Because?"

"Your problem wasn't that Sarah wouldn't come here." Holly pinned him with that needle-sharp look that couldn't be evaded. "Could it be that you thought having her come here was some kind of guarantee of her commitment?"

"I never thought of it that way, but I did think that once she moved she would have settled in." He made a face. "That was before she called Buffalo Gap Hicksville."

"But, Luc," Holly persisted. "You could have found work in the city if you really loved her. You could have given up your ranch." She nibbled on her bottom lip for a minute, a sure sign Holly had something else to say.

"Go ahead. You won't hurt my feelings," he said.

"I think you wanted Sarah to move here because you thought that would mean she really loved you," she said very quietly. "Maybe you didn't quite trust her."

Luc frowned, not liking what he heard but finding a grain of truth in Holly's words. "Why do you think that?"

"Because I made the same mistake." Her voice brimmed with sadness. "I hung on to my secrets until the last possible moment before I told Ron. That's not how trust works between people who love each other."

"You're saying you didn't really love him?" Luc found himself holding his breath as he waited for her answer and wondered why it mattered to him so much.

"I didn't love him enough to marry him." Holly's blunt admission surprised him. "First Corinthians 13 says that if you love someone you will be loyal to him no matter what the cost. You will always believe in him, always expect the best of him and always stand your ground in defending him. I couldn't do that for Ron."

"So another man will come along one day—" He stopped because Holly was shaking her head.

"No, I don't think it will be different with another man." Holly's lips tightened. "That's why I think God's plan is for me to remain single."

Luke was astounded by his need to scream "no." By the certainty that loving, motherly Holly deserved to marry and be the mom he knew she would be. By the urge to take her in his arms and assure her that God would never have created such lovingness in her if He hadn't intended her to share it with a family. Luc opened his mouth to object, but his response was cut off by the ring of the telephone.

Holly answered, listened for a moment then slowly hung up. When she turned to him, her face was ashen.

"That was Mayor Marsha. Henry's been hurt. He's at the hospital and he's asking for you."

Luc froze as fear grabbed him and held on.

"Come on, I'll drive you there." When he didn't, couldn't move, Holly grasped his arm and nudged him forward. "Come on, Luc. We need to go to Henry."

"But—" He could not voice all the things that could go wrong, that could steal this precious child from him. Fortunately, he didn't have to. Holly understood.

"Pray," she said quietly. "Pray and trust knowing that God's will is to do what's best for Henry."

As Holly drove him to the hospital, she talked about Henry's little foibles, the fun they'd had together and things she planned to do with him in the future.

"We need to take him on that fishing trip we promised," she said. "Maybe not tomorrow if he's injured, but we do have to make it happen, Luc. And we should also teach him to ride. Every kid should know how to ride a horse. And I want to make cookies with him."

Holly's list of activities kept him so busy during the drive into town that he almost stopped imagining the worst about Henry.

"Henry's going to need you to be strong for him, Luc," Holly said as she pulled up to the hospital.

"He's going to need you, too," Luc said. And that's when he knew that he wanted Holly there when Henry finally visited the ranch. He wanted all three of them together, safely enjoying this world God had created. Holly and Henry were part of his life now. And he couldn't lose either of them.

Chapter Five

"You had us so worried, Henry." Luc's pale, tense face bore witness to his words.

Holly grasped his arm and squeezed it to let him know she was there to support him, but also to help him calm down because she could see worry building in Henry.

"We're so glad you weren't badly hurt, Henry," she added. "Is your arm very painful?"

His bottom lip trembled as he shook his head, but he winced as the on-duty nurse pushed his sleeve up to bandage the razed skin.

"I'm okay," he said bravely.

Since they'd already heard from Mayor

Marsha that he'd raced into the street to save Hilda's cat and been bumped by a passing car, neither she nor Luc asked for more details. It was clear from the way Henry had latched on to Luc and not let go since they'd arrived that the boy had been badly frightened.

"There we go." Nurse Dora Cummings taped the last bit of gauze in place then handed Henry a sticker. "Good job, little man. In a day or two we'll take that off and put a small bandage on it. Pretty soon you won't even remember it was there."

"I appreciate the extra fussing over him, Dora," Holly whispered as they stood together near the door while Luc and Henry chatted.

"He's a cute kid. I think the worst damage he did was to scare himself. He'll be fine." The nurse frowned. "Say, did you check over that young girl that showed up at Family Ties?"

"Alice Something?" Holly shook her head. "Doc Treple did when she first showed up."

"No, she delivered yesterday. This one is Petra, Petra Stark."

"Never met her." Holly knew Dora was an excellent nurse. If her radar was up, there was good reason. "Something wrong?"

"I was at Family Ties today and I only saw her for a few minutes, but since I did something's been niggling at me. One of the other nurses did the workup that Abby always asks for before accepting a client at Family Ties. I checked it." Dora hesitated. "On the form Petra said she was thirty-six weeks along in her pregnancy."

"You think that's wrong," Holly said, understanding immediately.

"I think she's very close to giving birth but she's trying to hide it and I can't figure out why. You're better at getting patients to confide than I am." Dora's big smile stretched across her face. "I can never worm out all the details like you do. I thought maybe you could stop by, talk to her."

"I'll try." She thought for a moment. "I drove in with Luc and I'm not sure if he's in a hurry to get back, but if I can't see her tonight then I'll stop by tomorrow," Holly promised. "I have a couple of quilts to drop off anyway."

"I heard you'd volunteered to do quilts for each child Family Ties arranges adoptions for. That's generous. I love your baby quilts. I hope I get to see your latest one before it's gone. One is more adorable than the next."

"Thank you. But don't worry, I'll have pictures. I'll probably bore you to tears," Holly said, basking in the compliment.

"Your quilts would never bore me. I'm going to hire you to make me one if I ever manage to get pregnant." For a moment a flicker of uncertainty washed through her eyes.

"You will. At the right time." Holly wrapped an arm around Dora's shoulder and squeezed. "And you won't hire me because I'll give you one for a baby gift. Any special orders?"

"Anything you make will be perfect. Thank you, Holly." Dora glanced at her patient. "Tell Hilda the doctor says to keep Henry quiet tonight. He bumped his head and I think he still feels a bit woozy, though he won't admit it. There's no concussion and he should be fine by morning." After a wave for Henry she hurried away to tend to another patient.

As Holly turned she noticed Hilda emerge from another part of the emergency ward. Her face was pale and she was holding her hand to one hip. Before Holly could ask, Hilda explained that she'd hurried after Henry, tripped and injured herself. She was clearly weepy and began fussing over Henry's care.

"What if he needs me in the night and I can't get up those stairs?" Hilda said in a fretful tone.

"That would be awful," Holly agreed. She waited a moment then said, "Maybe, just for one night, Henry should go for a sleepover at Luc's." She waited with bated breath for Hilda's objections. None were forthcoming. In fact, Hilda looked relieved. "I don't know Luc's plans, but we could ask him. If you'd like?"

"I think I would like that," Hilda said with a heavy sigh. "And maybe Henry could stay two nights. I believe I'll need that long to get myself truly mobile."

"No one wants you to overtax, Hilda. Let's go see if Luc can manage it." Holly linked her arm in the older woman's and led her to Luc. She explained the situation, stifling a smile as she noted the joy now lighting his eyes and how quickly it spread to Henry who clung to his hand. "So we were wondering, do you think you could manage a couple of nights? Today's Friday so maybe until Sunday?" She waited for Hilda's nod.

"I'd be very glad to help you out, Hilda. Do we need to check with Abby first?" Luc politely waited for Hilda's response but Holly could see his anticipation.

"I've already phoned her to meet me here. She'll want to know about Henry's accident." A worried look filled Hilda's tired eyes. "I just hope she doesn't think I'm too old to handle him. I know I should have gotten to him sooner but…"

"Things happen with kids, Hilda. You know that." Holly hugged her. "You're doing a fine job of watching Henry. Abby will tell you that, too," she said as the owner of Family Ties hurried toward them.

After an explanation, Abby agreed Luc was the perfect answer in this situation. So half an hour later Holly and Luc were helping Henry load an overnight bag into Holly's jeep.

"Would it be okay if you two stop for a milk shake while I visit someone at Family Ties?" Holly asked them. Huge grins told her the two males would have no problem with that. As she watched them enter the café, a wistful thought flitted through her heart.

Luc would have Henry. But who would she have?

Holly knew of no way to soothe the ache inside except to pray for God to heal it. Then she walked into Family Ties to see the newest guest Dora had mentioned. Petra Stark sat in the living room. Holly fiddled around rearranging the quilts as she studied the girl and her movements. Petra certainly looked like she was further along in her pregnancy than thirty-six weeks.

"Hi," Holly greeted her, introducing herself and explaining her role. "I'm the nurse practitioner for Family Ties. We haven't met yet but I wanted to stop by and say welcome. I'll come to see you officially on Monday. We can chat then."

"About what?" Petra asked in a guarded tone.

"Anything you like. I'm here to help with whatever you need." Holly studied the young blonde while mentally assessing the tiny stress lines around her eyes. "Finding it hard to sleep?"

"Yes. The baby seems to be kicking me constantly. I can't sleep much at all." Petra nodded after Holly made some suggestions. "I'll try that," she said.

"Good. Here's my card. You call me if you want to talk or for any other reason and we'll set up a time to meet. If the baby starts coming, you call me right away."

"Oh, that won't be for a long time," Petra said, but her gaze didn't meet Holly's.

Holly walked out the door of Family Ties with a troubled heart. How could she help this girl if she couldn't get the truth?

"Is everything all right?" Luc rose from his seat on the top step. "You look concerned."

"I always am with a new patient and this one seems disinclined to tell me the truth. It's hard to help when someone won't trust you." She sighed then frowned at him. "You look worried, too. Where's Henry?"

"He finished his milk shake fast and needed something to do so I taught him to play a game on my phone. He's in the car," Luc said, pointing to Henry's dark head barely visible through the car window. "He's fine. It's not that." Luc raked a hand through his short hair, his dark eyes brooding.

"What is it then?" she asked, pushing back the weariness that swamped her.

"It's kind of embarrassing to admit," Luc muttered. Then he looked her straight in the eyes, dots of red coloring his prominent cheekbones. "I spent so long trying to figure out how to get him to my place. Now that he's coming, I don't know what to do with him. I'm scared, Holly."

"You can't be scared of Henry." She laughed but smothered it immediately as she realized how serious Luc was. It was odd to see the big rancher so unnerved by a little boy, but it was also endearing, and somehow sweet that he cared so much. "What's bothering you?"

"What if I do or say the wrong thing?" he said hesitantly. "Henry isn't my son yet. What if I do something that damages my case? What if I somehow hurt him or make a mistake with him? I couldn't stand that."

Luc looked so miserable that Holly had to reach out and pat his shoulder.

"Luc, nobody is born knowing how to be a parent. It's trial and error for everyone." She smiled, hoping to ease his anxiety. "I tell my prenatal classes that if you love the child and keep his best interests at the forefront of your mind, you won't go far wrong."

"I know but—" He hesitated before he continued. "Could you come over tomorrow morning and have breakfast with us? That might ease things."

"Sorry. I can't." She drew her hand away, wishing with all her heart that she could be there to watch Luc form tighter connections with Henry. "I just got a text and agreed to reschedule two prenatal appointments for tomorrow morning. I won't be free till noon or so."

"But what will I do with him until then?" Luc said in a panicked voice.

"What kind of things did you envision doing with your son?" She smiled at him, coaxing him to remember, hating to see this strong man so vulnerable. "Come on, Luc. You've talked about adopting Henry. Now's not the time to get cold feet. In fact, this is probably the perfect time to try the things you want to do with him when you adopt him. Show him what you love," she said quietly. "He'll love it, too."

"I guess that's my biggest fear," he admitted in a soft, hesitant tone. "Maybe Henry won't like my life. Sarah didn't."

"Are you kidding? Cowboys are Henry's heroes. To him you're the best thing since bubble gum." Holly shook her head at him. "You just wait, Luc. He's going to dive head-long into whatever you show him. But if he doesn't, you'll find something else, right?

Because Henry is the son you've always wanted."

Luc nodded. Then without warning he leaned forward and pressed a kiss against her forehead. "You're a good friend, Holly."

She gulped, utterly unnerved by that soft kiss and yet deeply moved that this strong, competent man needed her. It took a second to get her happy-go-lucky mask in place so Luc wouldn't see how deeply he'd affected her.

"Stop worrying and concentrate on the fun you'll have. This is what you prayed for. God's answered your prayer. Enjoy it." She smothered a yawn and thought how often she did that around Luc. He was going to start thinking of her as a doddering old spinster.

"Come on," he said. "You need to get home. I'll drive you back to the house and pick up my truck."

"Yes," she agreed. "Then you can take Henry home and tuck him up in that spare room you fixed up especially for him." She knew Luc had recently painted and installed new carpeting.

"I'm looking forward to that," he admitted in a soft voice that brimmed with yearning.

"You've got two whole days with Henry." Holly smiled at him. "You asked about God's will. Well, He's in control of everything so why not relax and enjoy this time with Henry and leave the future to God."

As they drove home, Holly decided that she was going to take her own advice, even if she had to sneak time from her sewing to spend it with Luc and Henry. She could sew anytime, but spending time with these two special guys was not to be missed.

"So we can have scrambled eggs with toast or pancakes," Luc offered. "Which one sounds good?"

"Scrambled eggs with toast and ketchup *and* pancakes," Henry decreed.

"Excellent." Though the boy showed no sign that last night's injuries still bothered him, Luc had decided to go with less ambitious activities today. He just hoped he could keep Henry interested.

He had barely begun cracking eggs into

the hot pan when a knock on the door made him pause. His heart gave a bump of relief when Holly stepped through the door. He'd wished she'd show up but didn't want to get his hopes up. Funny how with Holly on hand he felt less likely to botch the job of entertaining Henry.

"Have you eaten?" he asked. "We've decided on scrambled eggs and pancakes." Then he remembered. "I thought you had appointments this morning?"

"I did. Listen, lazybones, I was up way before you. I've been to Family Ties, had some cancellations at my office and now I have the rest of the day to myself." She grinned at him as if this was the best place she could imagine being on a sunny spring morning, then leaned down to tweak Henry's nose. "Hi, buddy."

When Holly turned her head and smiled at Luc, her joyous smile made his stomach clench. Belatedly, he realized smoke now filled the room from his overheated pan.

"I'll take an egg and some toast since

you're offering," she said, wrinkling her nose. "But I prefer my toast *not* black."

"Ha-ha. I didn't hear your car." Luc glanced out the window. The palomino gelding she'd named Babycakes stood placidly under a poplar tree, munching on freshly sprouted grass. "Oh, you rode."

"You talked about teaching Henry to ride, so I thought I'd be ready in case that's what you'd planned. Babycakes is always good to go."

"Really? You're sticking with that dumb name for that magnificent animal?" Luc made a face then got on with his cooking.

"He's a big baby, Luc. The name suits him." She chucked Henry under his chin and mussed his hair. "How're you feeling?"

"I'm good." Henry's eyes widened. "You mean we could ride a *horse*?"

"Yes, a horse." Holly giggled. "You're sure not going to ride Sheba," she joked, petting Luc's dog who rested under the table. "She's expecting puppies."

Luc had planned something else but if riding was what Holly wanted, that's what they'd do. Why was it she only had to look at him and he'd do anything she asked? He knew the answer. He'd promised Marcus he'd do his best to keep Holly happy and he had no intention of reneging on that promise.

"How about if I make toast while you cook the eggs and pancakes. And Henry can set the table." Holly waited for his nod then got to work.

Luc's kitchen filled with her laughter at Henry's newest knock-knock jokes. She told him a couple of her own and answered his endless questions with patience and humor. Mom Holly at her best.

Luc managed not to scorch the eggs or the pancakes, but it wasn't easy. His attention kept drifting to Holly with her glowing face. She didn't need cosmetics to make her more beautiful. She was already the most gorgeous woman he'd ever seen and it wasn't just a skin-deep beauty.

Though Luc didn't know what drove Holly to keep sewing, he did know how much she loved it. He could hardly have missed the mounds of fabric cut out in odd shapes piled on her dining room sideboard. He'd carefully avoided the quilt frame hogging a big corner of her living room, too. Holly was a woman with plans. She had things to do.

Yet she'd given up her beloved sewing to be here for him, to help him with Henry. That touched a spot deep inside him and Luc felt a rush of…something. Unwilling to define that feeling right now he slid the pile of fluffy golden eggs onto a plate and called the others to sit down. After a short grace, Luc leaned back and watched the pair dig into their breakfasts before his stomach rumbled and he attacked his own.

Henry was still gorging on pancakes when Holly pronounced the meal delicious and pushed her half-empty plate away.

"If it was so delicious, why did you pour a cup of ketchup on your eggs and then leave some?" he asked, delighted to see a flush of red staining her cheeks. She always seemed so in control.

"Me 'n Holly like ketchup," Henry explained, the red sauce smeared all over his face next to the syrup. "On everything."

"Except chocolate ice cream." Holly winked at Luc. "I don't like ketchup on that."

When Henry giggled, Holly joined him. A certainty filled Luc. This was going to be a wonderful day because of Holly. Out of the blue, a thought struck him. If he was looking for a wife, Holly would be the standard he'd use to measure her against.

But of course he wasn't getting married.

Once the dishes were in the dishwasher, Luc conferred with Holly because her advice was always good and because she had medical experience.

"Henry doesn't look to be hurting." Luc used his quietest voice while the boy lavished affection on Luc's dog. "But just in case, maybe he should ride in front of me to the stream?"

"Excellent idea," Holly agreed. "I wore my swimsuit just in case you'd planned to go there. The water might be chilly but—"

"Might be chilly?" Luc said drolly and arched one eyebrow.

"Okay, it will be frigid." She shrugged, unable to suppress her grin. "So?"

"Yeah, we're tough ranch people." He flexed a biceps, trying to look manly. "We can handle a little chill." He growled and bent over like a football player intent on sacking the quarterback.

He was acting silly. But Holly didn't seem to mind. In fact, she was growling, too, and encouraged a freshly-washed Henry to do the same. That was what Luc had always admired about Holly. No matter what the game, she always joined in.

"Let's go saddle up, pardner," he said to Henry, whose eyes stretched wide.

"What's a pardner?" Henry asked as they walked to the horse barn. "Is it like a partner?"

"Exactly the same," Luc assured him. "It's just a different way of saying it."

Henry hesitated in the barn doorway.

"What's wrong, bud?" Luc crouched down, saw the confusion in Henry's dark brown eyes.

"I don't think I can be your pardner." Henry's round face brimmed with misery.

"Why's that? Don't you like it here?" Luc

voiced his worst fear. "Don't you like me?" He hated asking but it was better to get it said out front, though saying those words made him cringe. What if—

Lord, help.

"It's not that," Henry rushed to reassure. "I love you and Holly. You're the nicest people I know." He glanced up at Holly and tried to smile but it was a poor effort. "I wish I could stay here forever."

"Then what's the problem?" Luc glanced at Holly and shrugged, trying to tell her without words that he was at a loss to understand what was going on.

To his dismay, Holly said nothing. She simply watched him for a moment then her glance strayed to her horse. Something in Luc's brain clicked.

"Henry," he said quietly, taking the boy's small hand in his. "Is it the horses? Are you afraid of them?"

Henry's head bobbed once.

"There's nothing to be afraid of. Horses are very gentle." Luc squeezed Henry's hand but the look on the boy's face told Luc it would take more than a few words to soothe his fears. He glanced at Holly again but she simply smiled and nodded, as if to encourage him.

"Can't we do something else?" Henry asked in a plaintive tone.

"Well, we could. But I really think you'd love our little creek. Holly's been going there since she was a kid." Luc saw a new frown appear.

"But I can't swim!" Henry wailed, looking ready to cry.

"Are you kidding me?" Luc touched his cheek then shook his head. "Henry, everyone can swim. They just have to learn how."

"Will you teach me?" Half-worried, half-excited, Henry shifted from one foot to the other.

"Maybe. If the water's warm and you want to. Or we could fish. What do you think, Holly?" he asked, trying to draw her into this. "I've been wanting a good feed of fish for ages."

"Either one sounds good to me." She crossed

her arms and tilted back on the heels of her cowboy boots.

Luc tossed her a frustrated look then turned his attention back to the boy he hoped would one day be his son. Maybe by then he'd be better at figuring out this kid. "Do you like to fish, Henry?"

"I don't know. I never did it." Worry had overtaken Henry's excitement. "Maybe we should stay here."

"I'll tell you what. Let's ride up to the creek and see if you like it. You don't have to ride a horse on your own," Luc explained, interrupting his objections. "We're pardners. You can ride in front on me on my horse. Dillyboy is a great horse. Very safe and gentle. He and I have gone lots of places together."

"Dillyboy?" Henry frowned. "You said Holly's horse had a silly name but Dillyboy is silly, too."

"I know. I bought him from a little girl." Luc made a face then pretended to sneak a look at Holly before he leaned close to Henry and whispered, "Her name was Dibby."

"Dibby and Dillyboy?" Henry's grin spread.

"See what I mean? I should probably change his name," Luc said, immensely relieved that Henry was no longer frowning. "Come on, I'll introduce you."

Very aware of Holly trailing behind them, Luc led the boy into the barn and to Dillyboy's stall. With great hesitation Henry touched his fingers to the stallion's crest and let them rest there a moment while he gathered his courage. Then he climbed on a bale, slid his hand upward, past Dillyboy's poll and between his ears to his forehead.

The horse whinnied and bent his head lower for a good rub which, when he understood, Henry willingly gave. His grin stretched wide when he touched Dillyboy's muzzle and the horse neighed his appreciation. But when Dillyboy dipped his head lower and nudged it against Henry's chest his smile drained away.

"He's going to eat me." Henry pulled back.

"No way. He's checking your shirt for carrots. He loves them." Luc walked over to a box where he always kept a few carrots. "Want to feed him?"

Henry thought about it for a moment then tentatively agreed. He took the carrot and held it out. Dillyboy couldn't reach and immediately stamped his foot.

"He won't hurt you, Henry," Luc explained. "But he can't reach the treat you're offering and he doesn't like that. Just hold it in the palm of your hand and he'll scoop it up."

Henry did and crowed with delight when the horse snatched the carrot and gobbled it up. Without asking the excited boy raced to the box, grabbed another carrot and repeated the action. After the third one, Luc called a halt.

"We don't want to stuff him. We need Dillyboy to give us a ride, remember." Slowly, patiently, careful to make sure Henry understood, he showed him how to prepare the horse for a ride. "You can sit here, in front of me, and I'll ride in the saddle."

"We're too heavy," Henry worried.

"No. Dillyboy has a silly name but he is very strong." Luc tightened the cinch the last millimeter, patted his horse's flanks then turned to Henry. "Ready?"

"I—I guess." He looked dubious when Luc swung up into the saddle but bravely accepted Holly's help to get settled on the horse in front of Luc.

Henry's face stayed tight and tense for several moments, until Luc had walked the horse out of the barn. He squealed when Luc nudged Dillyboy into a slow canter and squealed again when they drew to a stop by Holly's horse.

"Okay?" Luc asked him, sharing a look with Holly who gave a thumbs-up.

"Can we go faster?" Henry wanted to know.

"One step at a time," he cautioned, loving Henry's enthusiasm. "Hey, I forgot something. Stay here for a minute." He dismounted and handed the reins to Holly. "I'll be right back."

"We'll be here," she said, winking at Henry. "And, Luc?"

He stopped, turned back to her.

"Good job." A soft smile curved her pretty lips. "You'll make a wonderful father."

"Thanks." Luc strode back into the house to retrieve the picnic lunch he'd packed earlier. His heart sang with joy at Holly's words. He could do this. He could be a father.

As long as Holly was around to nudge him forward.

What would he do without Holly?

Chapter Six

"Thanks for letting me tag along today, Luc. It's been a long time since I've had so much fun." Holly's sides ached from laughing. She collapsed on a rock by the creek.

"Thanks for coming," Luc said.

She studied him, savoring the sheen on his face, clearly visible since he'd removed his Stetson.

"I thought I was in shape," he said, huffing as he sat down. "But clearly chasing a little boy all through this glade never figured in my fitness routine." He grimaced. "Henry, on the other hand, seems to be suffering not a whit from his accident yesterday. He's like one of your dad's buzzing bees."

"Kids recover amazingly well. You were great teaching him to swim." She was so proud of the way Luc accepted Henry's many fears and worked through each one.

She knew it hadn't been easy for Luc to overcome Henry's fear of actually immersing himself in running water, but she'd watched the cowboy draw on his incredible patience. Even though his lips pinched in frustration a couple of times, he'd pushed it back, inventing little games to get Henry used to the water until he'd finally managed to float a short distance on his own.

"I persisted because of something from my childhood," he said in a low voice.

"Oh?" Holly appreciated Luc's awareness of Henry standing fifty feet away, skipping pebbles over the water. He'd modulated his voice so the boy wouldn't hear.

"I saw another foster kid die when he was twelve because he couldn't master his fear of the water." Luc's face tightened. "It was such a needless thing. All kids should know how to swim and what to do if they get into trouble in the water."

Holly noted his fervent tone, surprised by it. She'd never have labeled Luc as passionate about things; he was always laid-back and comfortable. She liked this other side of him, admired his stance as a champion for kids. A lot.

"I've been thinking of what we were talking about." Holly smiled at his puzzled look. "God's will."

"Oh, yeah." His wry grin touched her heart. "We've talked about so many things I didn't connect for a minute. Did you come up with any answers?"

"No answers, but I remembered something." She paused, startled to realize that he was right. They did talk about a lot of things. As friends did. "It was a sermon I heard a long time ago, when I was in training." She deliberately looked away from him, not wanting to release too much information about her time in Toronto.

"Oh, yeah?" Luc's gaze was on Henry, making sure he was all right.

"The pastor said that if you were unsure about God's will for you and couldn't get the answers you needed, the best thing was to prayerfully keep moving forward with your plans." Holly squinted into the sun, trying to remember the exact words. "He said that if God wanted you to move in a different direction, He'd show you a new way."

"Makes sense." Luc pulled the stem off a blade of grass and worried it between his teeth as he gazed up at the clouds that floated past. "So you think I should keep on with my plans to adopt Henry and if God doesn't want that, He'll make it so I can't adopt?"

Holly nodded, but in her heart a bubble of fear grew. Luc had so much invested in Henry. His heart primarily, but he'd also planned, worked and now reached out to host the boy. If the adoption didn't go through, both he and Henry were going to be heartbroken.

That was where she came in, Holly decided. As his friend, her job was to help, maybe even protect Luc as much as she could.

"I had a phone call this morning," Luc murmured. When he didn't look directly at her, Holly frowned. "From Sarah."

She tamped down the immediate rush of anger. Luc wanted her friendship, not her judgment. For all she knew, he might still love her.

Listen, Holly. That's all he wants from you.

"Oh," she said, trying to sound noncommittal. "Is everything okay?"

"Not really." Luc threw away the stem he'd been chewing and sat upright. After congratulating Henry on a great stone throw he said, "She apologized for what she said. Apparently she'd had a big disappointment at work and says she took it out on me. She wants to come visit the ranch. She hinted about us maybe getting back together."

"Oh." Holly gulped, filled with loathing at the idea of Luc being tied to what sounded to her like a selfish woman. But she was there as his sounding board, she reminded herself again. "Is that what you want?"

"No." He shook his head to emphasize his rejection. "I'm not leaving my ranch and I don't want a part-time wife who lives miles away. I don't want to get together on week-ends and holidays. And where would kids fit in?"

"It could work, Luc. You could make it work if you wanted it enough." *Please don't want it.*

"Maybe, but I keep thinking about my buddies. If their marriages didn't work when they were together, both working on it, how good a marriage could it be when the couple doesn't share their everyday world?" He froze. "Hang on a second."

Holly watched him rise and jog over to Henry. He hunkered down beside the boy and said something that had Henry nodding agreement. Luc pulled a roll of candy out of his pocket, and Henry sat down on a big rock to enjoy his treat.

"Sorry. I figured he was about to take off after that squirrel." Luc sat back down. "Where was I?"

"Compromise," Holly told him.

"I don't want to compromise." Luc held her gaze, his own dark and intense. "I realized as I was talking to her that I don't want to sink everything I have into a relationship that I think is already doomed to failure. Ever since our breakup I've struggled to focus on not settling."

"So you told her no?" Holly fought to keep her voice even, striving for impartiality though inside she was cheering his decision.

"Yes." He frowned. "I don't want to hurt Sarah. I just don't love her anymore, if I ever did. And I'm beginning to doubt that. I think it's a blessing we broke up. I'm not the guy she needs. I love ranching. I don't want to do it part-time. And I do want to adopt Henry."

"Are you sure, Luc?" She wondered if he'd regret his decision later, especially if the adoption didn't go through. "Maybe if you thought about it a little more—"

"No. I'm certain." Luc heaved a sigh. "I've realized a few things since we split up, things you've helped me see more clearly."

"Me?" Holly squeaked.

"Yes, you, Holly Janzen." He reached out and brushed the end of her nose with his finger. "You take a no-holds-barred approach to life. You press through the tough parts, like your dad's passing and Ron's departure, and you don't settle. And then there's your sewing thing."

"My sewing 'thing'?" she repeated and wrinkled her nose at him.

"I don't know what else to call it." Luc grinned when she rolled her eyes. "But anyway, I watch you keep pursuing that. You're passionate about it and you don't let things like lack of space or anything else stop you from doing what you love."

"There's a difference between sewing and marriage," she said, surprised and pleased by his comments.

"Is there? The Bible says to press toward the mark of the high calling. It doesn't say settle for compromise." He crossed his arms over his chest and leaned back. "Breaking up with Sarah really hurt, maybe more because she's not the first one who's rejected me because I live on a ranch and horses are my life."

That was news to Holly but she decided not to ask him about it, not right now anyway.

"I don't want to open myself up to that

rejection again, Holly." His voice emerged low with an ache underlying the words. "It's like being gutted. All the things I love she hates. No matter how I compromise I won't ever feel like I'm enough."

"Then you're right to refuse her." She saw Luc almost every day yet she hadn't realized what he was going through. He'd been there for her so often. But when had she been there for him? Friendship was supposed to work two ways.

"Is that the way you feel about Ron?" His quiet, hesitant voice made her look at him.

"I expected too much of Ron," she said softly. "I realize that now."

Silence fell between them as they watched Henry throw larger and larger stones into the water, laughing at the splash they made.

"He's wonderful," Luc murmured. And Holly agreed.

"I learned something new about adoptions," she said, hoping he wouldn't think her nosy.

"Tell me." Luc shifted slightly, alert as

Henry moved near the horses, picking wild-flowers.

"An article I read said it makes a big impression on the powers that be when you know the child's routine and have already made adjustments for it," Holly told him. "Like knowing his favorite games—"

"Checkers," Luc shot back in a dry tone. "I don't know where he learned to play, but he's very good at it."

"Oh. Good," she said, startled that Luc had already gained this information. "It also said that if you talk to his caregiver and find out what his normal routine is you will be better prepared to make adjustments."

"I spoke to Hilda while you were helping Henry pack to come here." Luc held up his hand and began to tick off items on each finger. "I know he sometimes wakes calling for his brother and that he likes a snack before he goes to bed. His favorite color is blue. His favorite food is French fries and his best memory is of him and his brother biking in a park."

"Ah, that explains the blue bedroom." Luc

was miles ahead of her, Holly realized as she returned his smile. But she wanted to alert him to everything she'd learned. "It also said you should have a financial plan in mind for his future."

"I set up what I call my adoption fund for that purpose," Luc told her. "I've been putting a little extra in it since I met Henry because someday I'd like to invite his brother out here. Nothing's carved in stone, I just thought that maybe when Finn gets out his being here might help Henry, though I'm not sure exactly when that will be."

"You've thought of everything." She was in awe of his foresight.

"The debacle with Sarah taught me to consider every angle." He shifted uneasily and made a face. "You know, I've been meaning to talk to you about something. Abby gave me a document with a whole list of questions to answer. I'm supposed to have it done by Monday but I haven't even started."

"Why not?" Holly could see how difficult the admission was for him. "Tell me," she said quietly.

"I'm scared to answer them. It feels like some kind of trap. If I answer wrong, I could lose Henry." He looked at her, his brown eyes shadowed. "Adopting him means so much. I can't lose him because I didn't answer a question the right way."

"Oh, Luc." She moved closer and laid her hand on his. "Have some faith. This little boy needs a home. You have a home. And you have a lot of friends in Buffalo Gap. One of them is Abby. She's not going to trick you. She's just doing her job so that when you get Henry, nobody will be able to undo that. And you've got God on your side, remember."

Luc studied her for a long time. When at last he spoke, Holly saw past the words to his sincerity and tried to keep from blushing.

"How do you stay so positive, Holly? Don't you ever get overwhelmed by everything?" He answered his own question with a shake of his head. "No, I guess you don't. Even during your dad's illness and after he died, I never saw you at a loss. You always seemed confident things would work out."

"I'm not always confident," she said, half-annoyed that he saw her as some paragon of virtue. "But I don't see the value in repeatedly voicing the direness of my situation. Maybe it's my profession. Nurse practitioners are trained to deal with issues and move on."

"It's not only that. It's more that I see a confidence inside of you," Luc said. "An assurance that God is in control and He'll work things out."

"Isn't that what the Bible promises?" she asked in exasperation. She was so tired of this perfect image. But if anyone knew how far from perfect she was, maybe they'd doubt her ability to do her job.

"I need to emulate your faith," he said.

"No, you don't," she said in exasperation. "I'm not perfect, Luc. I get as down as anyone else, mess up as badly as anyone, have as many doubts as anyone else. But in the end, God *is* in control, even when it doesn't seem like it. I try to remember that."

Suddenly Holly noticed that Henry had been watching them. She was pretty sure he'd overheard them because he was now walking toward them.

"Are you an' Luc fighting?" A frown marred Henry's smooth forehead.

"Nope, we're not." Luc smiled. "We're discussing. That means we're trying to find out what the other one thinks."

"Oh." Henry considered that for a moment before nodding. "Maybe you need Ms. Hilda's verse."

"Maybe we do." Holly shot Luc a sideways look then smiled to encourage the boy. "What's the verse, Henry?"

"I'll try to remember." Henry scrunched up his face. "'I leaned on You since I was borned...' I forget the rest." He sighed. "Ms. Hilda says it's from a song in the Bible."

"A psalm?" Holly asked, hiding her smile.

"Maybe." Henry shrugged. "It means God's been with you since you were a baby."

"It's a great verse. It does help our discussion." Luc's face beamed as he lifted a hand and smoothed it across Henry's brow. "Thank you very much."

"Welcome." Henry leaned against Luc's arm. "I'm hungry, Luc."

"Again?" Immediately Luc's face dropped. "But we've eaten everything I brought for lunch. I didn't realize—I should have known—" He stared at Henry, clearly blaming himself for not planning better.

"I had a hunch all that swimming and riding might make you hungry," Holly said. She grinned at Henry. "I've noticed that boys and men can eat a lot."

"That's 'cause we have to be strong, right, Luc?" Henry proudly flexed a puny bicep.

"Right." Luc studied Holly with a calculating look. "What's in your saddle pack? No, wait. I think I can guess. S'mores?" He gave a triumphant hoot when she nodded.

"And lemonade," she said.

"You just can't give up the chocolate, can you, Holly?" Luc's gaze felt like the sun, warming, cherishing her.

"Be glad about that," she said with a teasing growl. "Or I might not share."

"What's a s'more?" Henry asked.

"Oh, my boy, you have a real treat coming

if you've never had a s'more." Luc jumped up, held out a hand to Holly and when she grasped his, tugged her upright. "You and I are going to build a fire in that pit over there," he said to Henry. "And then Holly and I will introduce you to s'mores. You'll love them."

Henry studied Luc's every move, mirroring each action with one of his own. Slowly the two males built a tiny fire inside the metal rim of a tractor tire that Holly's dad had brought here when she was a small girl.

A pang shot through Holly's heart as she watched the two heads nearly touching as they fed the fire. That bittersweet moment stung so much she had to turn away and busy herself spreading the snacks over the makeshift table she and her dad had fashioned out of a tree stump when she was just a bit older than Henry.

She touched her fingers to the *HJ* carved into the corner of the top and suddenly the memories were too much. She tried to stop them, but in spite of her best efforts, a tear slipped down her cheek.

"What's wrong?" Luc murmured. She hadn't even seen him move and yet he was suddenly in front of her, tipping up her chin so he could look into her eyes. Without saying a word he gathered her into his arms and held her close, whispering words of comfort.

"He gave me such a wonderful childhood," she said through her tears, soaking Luc's shirt and not caring. "I never realized how hard he worked to be both mom and dad to me. I miss him so much."

"I know. But Marcus is in your heart and your soul." Luc's breath skittered across her skin, ruffling nerve endings that trembled at being so close to him. "Your dad will always be with you."

"Just like Jesus," Henry said, standing just beyond them, his gaze intent as it rested on them. "He said He'll always be with us, too."

"Yes, He did." Luc pulled back and peered into Holly's face. "Are you okay?" he asked softly.

"I'm fine. Just being a bit of a crybaby." She dashed away her tears and smiled at

Henry. "Thank you for reminding me, sweetheart."

"Can we make the s'mores now?" Henry asked. "'Cept I don't know how."

"First Luc needs to make us some sticks to roast our marshmallows." She found his gaze unnerving and quickly veered her focus back to her supplies on the table.

Luc was her very good friend. But he'd never held her before. Not even after her father's funeral. It felt like something in their relationship had changed, become more intimate. And that scared Holly.

She watched as Luc showed Henry how to choose the perfect roasting stick from a nearby poplar tree. When Henry had selected his, Luc quickly whittled down the twig and began shaping the point with his pocket knife while Henry watched and, as usual, asked questions.

It wasn't that Holly hadn't liked Luc's arms holding her, lending support. She had. Maybe too much. But she couldn't allow herself to dwell on how right it had felt. She couldn't afford silly girlish dreams about a cowboy on his horse because this wasn't a dream. Luc had told her time and again that he wasn't getting involved. His focus was on Henry.

So when the pair returned, she forced herself to smile as she slid the giant marshmallows onto their sticks and watched them roast the confections to a toasty brown. She had squares of chocolate on graham wafers ready and scooped up Henry's marshmallow before he lost it to the fire. She managed a carefree laugh with Luc when the boy tasted his treat and his eyes grew huge before he quickly asked for a second. And when Luc insisted she accept his marshmallow for her own treat, Holly thanked him, just as she always had done.

But deep inside the feeling that she'd soon be left out lingered like a blister. It wasn't anything the others did. It was more seeing how Luc and Henry bonded over the snack and later fishing that made her feel like a third wheel.

By the time the sun had sunk below the foothills, Henry drooped wearily. Holly just wanted to get home and mull over the day in private. That's when Luc's phone rang.

"Hi, Mayor… You do?… Oh." He paused, lifted his head and started at Holly. "Um, I guess I could though I don't know anything about hosting that kind of thing." Suddenly his eyes brightened. "Yeah, you're right. I could ask Holly. Okay, I'll do it. Bye." By the time he'd pocketed his phone Luc was grinning.

"You could ask Holly to do what?" A flicker of worry built inside her. She'd hate to say no to Luc, but she needed to put some distance between them to sort out her feelings.

"The mayor says that each month someone involved with Family Ties hosts a potluck supper. Since I'm a volunteer and hopefully soon-to-be a parent, she suggested I hold the next potluck, probably next week." Excitement shone in his brown eyes then dimmed. "But I don't know anything about potlucks. Marsha said I should ask you for help."

"The potlucks are fun," she said without thinking. Her mind raced with ideas. "I always thought a theme party would be fun.

Maybe a birthday theme? That could be a lot of fun. You sure have enough yard space."

"How would I do it?" Luc gave her that beseeching look that she never could resist. "Help me, Holly."

She'd gone and done it again, gotten herself involved when she was trying to opt out. She had a ton of sewing orders due, but they couldn't compare with the thrill of sharing hosting duties with Luc.

"Let's talk about it on the way back," she said, noticing how Henry dragged his feet. "Time to saddle up, Henry."

Moments later their horses were ambling toward Luc's ranch as Holly spouted potluck ideas left and right.

"You could print out birthday invitations," she said. "Specify birthday food so people will know what to bring. And you could supply dessert, which could be a big cake to celebrate everyone's birthday."

"Holly, I can't make a cake!" Luc cried, so loud that a sleeping Henry roused in the saddle in front of him.

"I made a cake with Ms. Hilda," Henry mumbled. "We could help you."

"A very good idea," Holly murmured. "Building bonds and all that." Luc frowned then nodded. "You could decorate the yard with balloons and make it look like a real party. People will love to bring their children because they won't have to find sitters."

"I'd need activities for the kids then." Luc frowned at her. "I don't think I'm much good at that."

"No time to learn like the present. After all, you're going to be a father," she reminded him with a wink.

They brainstormed all the way back. Only when they finally rode into the yard did Holly notice that dusk had crept across the ranch. By then Luc was really getting into the idea of hosting this party.

"I could have a bonfire and we could roast hot dogs," he mused aloud as he lifted Henry down and held the sleeping boy cradled in his arms. "Or do you think a fire would be too dangerous with kids around?"

"Why not discuss it with Abby? She'd

be able to give you the best advice." Holly lifted his saddle packs off the horse and carried them into his house, noting how Henry's arms had automatically moved to circle Luc's neck.

The sweet sight of this big gentle man cradling the little boy made Holly sigh.

"He's beat." She could hear Luc's fondness for Henry in his voice. "I'm going to put him straight to bed. He can shower in the morning."

"I'll leave you to it then," Holly said quietly, needing to be alone to decipher her unusual feelings. "Thank you for a wonderful day. I had so much fun. Thanks for sharing Henry with me."

She smiled at Luc but his answering smile did odd things to her stomach so she brushed a light hand across Henry's cheek before kissing it then hurried out the door before Luc could coax her to stay.

Holly rode home quickly, her horse comfortable on the familiar paths. Her brain kept replaying moments throughout the day, special moments she'd tucked away to savor, moments when Luc had seemed like the soul mate she'd once hoped Ron might be.

How wrong she'd been about Ron. Everything she thought she'd known, everything she thought she'd loved had been mistaken. And now, as she pondered the day she'd spent with Luc, she thought perhaps she understood why.

She hadn't really loved Ron. She'd never felt the peculiar, catch-your-breath reaction with Ron that she'd felt this afternoon. Nor had she felt it with the father of her child. Infatuation, yes. But how could she have thought that was love?

Holly had always known her mother hadn't loved her father. Otherwise, why would she have left? Maybe that was why Holly craved that solid, steadfast, there-no-matter-what love in her own relationship. Other people found it. Abby had it with Cade. So why couldn't she find it?

With Luc?

The question nagged at her as she curried the horse and put him away for the night.

Did she want a relationship with Luc? He

was her good friend, but he'd never been more than that. She'd never wanted him to be. Did she now? Was that the reason behind these unusual reactions to him?

Holly stepped inside her house. Her spirit dropped at the piles of fabric littering the dining room and the dream dissipated. Of course she didn't want a romantic relationship with Luc. She'd accepted that it was God's will for her to remain single so why was she asking herself these silly questions when she had tons of orders to sew and ship?

She brewed herself a cup of coffee and set to work finishing the late orders, muttering to herself as she sewed an incorrect seam and had to pick it out from the delicate lace dress meant for a baby dedication.

Wait a minute! This was work that had always lifted her spirit, made her happy. So why did it feel like a chore?

"This is what you do, Holly," she lectured out loud. "You make one-of-a-kind things for other people's kids. It's what you *love*," she emphasized.

That didn't help. A hank of glossy white

satin lay sprawled across the sideboard. She rose and walked toward it, sliding her sensitive fingertips down the length, luxuriating in its weight and richness. Perfect for a new baby at a family event where friends and loved ones gathered to support the baby's parents as they promised to raise their child to know God.

A well of longing erupted inside. Holly could not deny it. She wanted the husband, the family, the friends *and* the child. She'd tried to suppress it, pretended she didn't crave what everyone else had. But those yearnings wouldn't stay neatly tucked inside.

Okay, she could never have the child she'd birthed. That child had another family, another mother now. She'd made that decision knowing full well it was final.

"But I was just a kid. I didn't realize—"

There was no point in going over it all again. Nothing had changed. She was still alone. Luc was her friend, but he didn't want marriage. He'd made that very clear. She'd tried to find happily-ever-after with Ron, but he hadn't been able to excuse her behavior. What God-fearing man could forgive a woman for giving her baby away in order to save her reputation?

For a while today Holly had let herself get caught up in the idea of her own romance but it was just a mirage, not reality.

Holly took another sip of her coffee then set it aside and began sewing, forcing everything from her mind but the work she needed to complete to pay for her father's medical supplies and eventually the renovations for her sewing room.

God didn't intend for her to be a wife or a mother. It was time to put those dreams away.

Chapter Seven

"I've already made a potato salad and a garden salad, but are you sure I can't help with something else for your potluck tonight?" Hilda asked Luc as she rebuttoned Henry's shirt where he'd left a gap.

"Thanks, Ms. Hilda, but I have about a hundred lists. I've checked and rechecked and I think I—" Luc grinned at Henry. "I think *we've* got it covered."

"Well, okay then." Hilda smoothed Henry's cowlick then stepped back and nodded in approval before turning to study Luc. "I do think this 'birthday' potluck is such a wonderful idea. We who volunteer for Family Ties have never done a birthday theme before. It's going to be a fun night tonight, especially for Holly."

"Why Holly?" Luc asked, slightly confused.

"Because her birthday is tomorrow." She frowned at him. "Don't tell me you've forgotten the shenanigans Marcus went through to celebrate her special day?"

The thing was, Luc had forgotten.

"I remember when Holly was just a wee thing and her dad wanted to surprise her with a pony." Hilda chuckled. "The whole town was in on getting that little pinto pony to the ranch and hiding it so she wouldn't find it till morning."

"Her birthday is tomorrow." Luc checked his watch to confirm the date and frowned. How could he have forgotten? More to the point, what was he going to do to make it especially nice for Holly, not the least because she'd been there helping him prepare?

"You didn't remember?" Hilda frowned at him as if she suspected he was addled by the sun.

"How could I forget?" Luc said with a

laugh, as if he'd known all along. With sudden inspiration he asked, "Ms. Hilda, you don't have any strings of those fairy lights folks use at Christmas, do you?"

"Why, yes, I do. I have several boxes. I intended to put them up last Christmas but then I went on that trip and didn't have time so they've never been used. Why?" She inclined her head like a curious bird.

"May I borrow them? For the potluck tonight?"

"Well..."

It took a little explaining but finally Hilda approved his newest idea. Luc loaded the lights in his truck, thanked her for them then headed over to the bakery to add a birthday cake to his order and tell them Abby would pick it up. He wasn't taking any chances of making a cake that could ruin his party.

"You sure have a lot of errands." Henry trotted hard to keep pace as Luc led him through the five-and-dime store for balloons, some multicolored streamers and a bag of candy.

"Yes, I do. Hey, there's Mayor Marsha. I

need to talk to her." Luc handed him the items and gave him ten dollars to pay for it while he explained his change of plans to Marsha. "It's Holly's birthday tomorrow so I thought we'd turn tonight's potluck into a surprise party, if that's okay with you."

"Sounds like a fantastic idea," Marsha enthused. "It will make Holly's birthday less sad for this first year without her father."

"I know the town has some kind of phone list where one person calls the next. Could you use it to send some calls around so folks know we're celebrating her birthday?" Luc asked.

"Something special for Holly." Marsha gave Luc a knowing glance. "Leave it to me." She waggled her fingers goodbye before hurrying away. Luc stared at her disappearing figure, confused by that look.

"Here's the change," Henry said, tugging on Luc's pant leg to get his attention. "What's this candy for?"

"I'll explain later. Now we need to go to the florist." Once he picked out the flowers and arranged for them to be delivered to

Holly tomorrow morning, Luc drove back to his ranch mentally reviewing the tasks still to be done for tonight.

"What's my job?" Henry demanded when they arrived at the ranch.

"You fill this with the candy." He showed Henry how to ease the candy through the hole in the rainbow piñata he'd bought earlier. "While you work at that, I'm going to hang Ms. Hilda's lights."

"But you told Holly you weren't going to hang any lights for the potluck," Henry said. Looking suddenly bashful he added, "I heard you say that at church on Sunday."

"I wasn't going to hang them," Luc said, feeling a little bashful himself.

"So why are you?" As usual, Henry was full of questions.

Luc really liked his inquisitive side. Henry's desire to learn was refreshing, but Luc wasn't crazy about explaining his change of heart regarding the lights. Mostly because he hadn't yet figured out himself why it mattered so much. Judging by the look on

Henry's face, he wasn't about to leave the subject without getting an answer.

"Holly loves fairy lights. Since her birthday is tomorrow, I think we should do something extra special for her." Luc paused in unpacking the lights to glance at Henry.

Those big brown eyes held a steady bead on him. "You like Holly, don't you?"

"Yes," Luc admitted. "We're good friends."

"Holly has lots of friends," Henry said.

"She sure does," Luc agreed, thinking how true it was.

"Know why? 'Cause she makes people feel better." Henry returned to stuffing candy into the piñata.

"You mean with medicine?" Henry shook his head. Curious to hear his response Luc asked, "Why, then?"

"She makes them feel better inside." Henry patted his chest. "In here. She always smiles and says nice things and tries to help."

"Yes, she does." Luc couldn't smother his own smile as he draped the tiny lights from tree to tree, creating what would become an arbor of light after dark.

Holly certainly made him feel better inside but that was friendship. It didn't mean anything more. Slightly unsettled by the turn of his thoughts, Luc mentally listed all the reasons there could be nothing more than friendship between them.

Remember the hit to your ego when Sarah dumped you? Remember how hard it was to get back your self-esteem? Remember that hollow sick feeling in your stomach every time you went to some activity at church and realized you didn't fit in the couples' groups or the married groups anymore? That again you were a single man in a church full of families?

Luc remembered all of it. Too well. He could close his eyes and it would all come back, that feeling that he wasn't enough, that he had no pictures of his kids to proudly show off like other men, that he couldn't make teasing jokes about his wife.

But he didn't want a relationship, certainly not that stomach-turning reaction on realizing that the woman he'd trusted completely hated everything about him. It all rushed back like a tidal wave. No way would he risk going through all that misery again.

Yet, in a way, Luc didn't want to forget any of what he'd gone through because he didn't want to make the same mistake. He had no desire to pour his love into a relationship only to be dumped all over again.

At first he'd seen the breaking of his engagement as something terrible, but now he realized that it'd been a blessing. At least it had saved him from the same fate as his buddies. So did that mean his broken engagement had been part of God's will?

"You're not eating all those candies, are you, Henry?" he called, suddenly aware of the silence.

"Just two peanut butter ones. I love peanut butter." Henry's lips smacked. Luc squinted and saw streaks of chocolate and peanut butter smeared across his face, especially around his lips.

"Henry, it's not good for you to eat too many—" He cut off the reprimand when Henry tossed a candy at him.

"You like peanut butter, too." Henry selected another candy for himself with a sneaky grin.

"Yes, I do." Luc grinned and popped the chocolate in his mouth, almost laughing aloud at Henry's wit. "But that's enough. We don't want to spoil our supper."

"Just one more, okay?" The candy was in Henry's mouth before Luc could protest.

Luc gave the boy a stern look, and Henry went back to stuffing the piñata. Luc returned to stringing another set of lights. A tickle of laughter burst out as he envisioned Holly's surprise when she saw the lights twinkling above her tonight. He started to whistle and then paused. What was all this bubbly feeling about?

"Where are you going to hang the rainbow?" Henry asked.

"I don't know." Luc climbed down from his ladder, surveyed his work and nodded. It looked good and until they were switched on, Holly would never even guess he'd put them up. "Where do you think the piñata should hang?"

"Is it just for kids?" When Luc assured

him it was, Henry surveyed the yard then pointed. "Over there. Then they won't hit anyone if they miss."

"Excellent choice. Can you hold it while I hang it?" A few minutes later the rainbow gently waved in the warm afternoon breeze. "Good job, Henry."

"Is it gonna rain?" Henry asked, scanning the sky.

"No, that's not a rain sky. One day I'll teach you about clouds." Luc smiled at the very thought of such a delightful future. "Anyway we can't have rain on the night of our party for Holly," he chided as he tickled Henry under his ribs and then swung him in a circle. And surely nothing could stop his plans to adopt this precious boy.

They collapsed together on the ground. The feel of Henry in his arms, the sound of his giggles in his ears brought a lump to Luc's throat. Was there anything more blessed than a child's laughter? Wanting to enjoy every ounce of pleasure with Henry while he was here, Luc collapsed on the grass and lay back, pointing out the cloud formations to the almost-son pressed against his side.

It should have been perfection, but some niggling part of Luc wished Holly was here to share these moments with Henry and him.

"I hope I get to live here soon." Henry lay with his head tucked under Luc's arm.

"I hope so, too, Henry. I hope it more than anything." Luc sent up a prayer before he hugged him close. For the hundredth time he assured himself that adopting Henry had to be God's will.

"Do we have chores before the party?" Henry sat up when Luc nodded. "Should I change into my work clothes?"

"You know where they are?" Luc asked.

"In the closet in *my* room." Henry jumped to his feet. "I'll race you to the house."

"No rush," Luc told him, but he doubted Henry heard as he took off running to the room Luc had painted blue because Henry loved the color.

"I'm ready." Henry returned to the kitchen a few moments later proudly dressed in the baggy overalls and red plaid shirt Luc had bought him. He danced from foot to foot, clearly impatient. "Hurry, Luc. We don't want to be late for the party."

"How could we be late? It's going to be held here," Luc grumbled, dumping out his coffee after only a taste. "We can hardly miss it."

Truthfully, Luc felt the same excitement as Henry, but he couldn't decide if it was because of Henry's presence in his home or because Holly was coming. Probably both, he decided then thrust away the tiresome warning his brain kept offering about getting too close to Holly. How perfect that Henry seemed to love helping with jobs around the ranch.

They worked together companionably with Henry asking his usual plethora of questions. When chores were done they went inside to shower. Luc went first while Henry enjoyed one last candy that somehow hadn't made it into the piñata. Then it was Henry's turn to shower. When his squeaky tones warbled from the bathroom all the way to the kitchen where Luc was polishing his boots, Luc sat still and let the sound of it penetrate to his heart.

This is what I want, God.

He realized the only other time he'd felt this burst of joy was when he was with Holly. Luc's world came alive when Holly stopped by just as it did when he was with Henry.

"Lord, I love this kid," he said, his heart full. "Please let him move here soon. If that's Your will," he added after a second's thought. But how could this not be God's will? Henry needed a home and Luc needed Henry. And Holly would be there for both of them.

Luc was savoring that thought as he smoothed down Henry's cowlick when Holly drove into the yard.

"Remember what I said, Henry," Luc murmured.

"I know. It's a surprise." Henry grinned at him then took off running to meet Holly.

The exuberance and affection in their reunion brought a wave of emotion that made Luc gulp. Holly, clad in formfitting jeans and a white shirt, scooped Henry into her arms and swung him around. Luc's gaze was riveted on her face. Pure unadulterated joy rested there as she clung to Henry. Then she murmured something in his ear and leaned back to smile at his response.

Henry seemed just as enthralled with his arms wrapped around her neck. Holly tossed Luc a grin as she set Henry on the ground. That smile made Luc's evening suddenly brighter.

"We're going to have so much fun tonight," Holly said tweaking Henry's nose.

"I know." Henry's little chest puffed out with pride. "I helped Luc get ready."

Luc admired the way Holly crouched down to listen with rapt attention as the boy enthused about the things he and Luc had prepared. Holly could deny it all she wanted, but she was a natural mother.

Once or twice Luc opened his lips, ready to intervene when it seemed Henry would give away the secret. But Henry stopped in time, gave him a smile and changed the subject.

"What's going on?" Holly asked when Henry rushed off to greet a friend from school.

"He's excited about tonight. What did you

bring for the potluck?" Luc couldn't tear his eyes off her. She glowed, her cheeks pink, her blue eyes shining and her curls bobbing behind the white ribbon that held them off her face.

"I baked some fresh rolls. I hope they taste all right." Holly pointed to the big tray of golden buns she'd already set on the table.

"Why wouldn't they be okay?" he asked, suddenly realizing how hungry he was.

"Right in the middle of mixing them I got called into town for a delivery. Maxine Mallory had her baby this afternoon." She made a face, and he knew exactly what it meant.

"I'm guessing that was more of a production than the usual birth?" Luc smirked when she rolled her eyes.

"Everything is more of a production with Maxine." She gave him a wry look then shook her head. "They now have another son, which makes four. A darling sweet child that yelled once when he arrived before settling into his mother's arms. Seven pounds seven ounces. Healthy and happy."

"That's the outcome you like," he said, knowing it was true.

"Yes," Holly agreed haltingly. "It was just a bit disconcerting that Maxine had such a short labor, especially when her due date is still two weeks off and there's nothing in Seth Treple's notes to indicate he thought she would be early. I don't like surprises like that."

The tightness of Holly's voice told Luc she'd been worried for her patient. He required no explanation for her expressions. A breathless sigh meant Holly was tired. Tiny frown lines on her smooth forehead told him she'd probably been chastised by the very vocal Maxine. The slump of her shoulders said she'd given her best for mom and baby. The twinkle in her eye meant she was thrilled she'd been there to help deliver the baby and was now looking forward to a relaxing evening.

Luc blinked. When had this communication without words happened? Could Holly read him as easily?

"What can I do to help, Luc?" She ruffled Henry's hair when he returned.

"Me 'n Luc already did it all," Henry told her, stretching tall. "It's for you to relax."

Luc had never been more proud of his would-be son.

"Really?" Holly glanced from Henry to Luc.

"Henry's right. We've done most of it." He shrugged at her surprised look. "Now what we need is a hostess to make everyone feel welcome."

"I'm your girl." She shrugged as if that was such a little thing to ask. Holly was a born hostess. "But if you need something else, ask."

"Your work is about to begin." Luc inclined his head toward the road. "Isn't that Cade's truck?"

"Meeting and greeting is exactly what I feel like doing tonight." She tossed him a smile before hurrying toward Abby to take one of the twins. "These two are growing like weeds," Luc heard her say. "I don't suppose they'll fit the outfits I made for very long. I better get sewing again."

Was he the only one who glimpsed the rush of longing filling Holly's face as she held the baby? A second later that look was gone, hidden behind her ever-present smile, leaving Luc even more curious about the sewing that filled her life.

"You're using my kids as an excuse to sew something new," Abby teased as she set the twins in a playpen Cade set up.

Certain the children were settled and happy with their toys, Holly touched Abby's arm.

"Do you have a moment? I've been meaning to talk to you but it's been so hectic."

Luc exchanged greetings with Cade who was quickly drawn away by Henry who wanted to show him the piñata. Concerned by the intensity of Holly's voice, Luc lingered to listen in on the conversation.

"I've been trying to get Petra to confide in me, but it's not going well." Holly rubbed the back of her neck. "She's hiding something about her pregnancy and I'd prefer to know what before she goes into labor."

"You think she's that close?" Abby asked.

"Pretty sure." Holly nodded. "I saw her again today. The baby's dropped."

"But she keeps telling me she has almost a month to go." Abby sighed. "Running Family Ties isn't as easy as I thought it would be. I appreciate your help, Holly."

"Anytime. Family Ties is making a real difference to moms who have nowhere to go to have their babies. I'm really glad you decided to make sheltering them a part of the Family Ties ministry. It takes a lot of stress off the mother when she knows she has a safe place to stay until the birth." Holly handed Abby a glass of the punch Luc had made earlier. "Or would you rather have coffee?"

"This is great." Abby drew him into the conversation. "Luc, your place looks wonderful. I see you've added a tree swing for Henry."

"And a sandbox. Isn't that cover ingenious?" Holly enthused with a wink at him.

"Luc built it so it keeps the sand clean and dry when Henry's not using it."

"He's a lucky boy." Abby's gaze tracked Henry's progress as he raced around the yard pretending to be an airplane. "He's certainly loosening up."

"Does that mean the adoption will go through?" Luc asked, wishing he didn't sound so needy. He knew Holly worried he was investing himself too deeply in an outcome that might not happen.

"Things are progressing very well," was all Abby would say. "We have three new boys to find homes for," she told them. "But they're babies. Are you interested, Luc?"

"I want to adopt Henry," he said, meeting her gaze and holding it. "I have to see that through."

"Committed, I see. Good for you. Oh, here comes Hilda. And Mayor Marsha." Abby turned away to speak to her friends.

"I'm always intimidated by that woman," Luc said to Holly in a low tone.

"Who? Mayor Marsha?" Holly chuckled. "She's been a real blessing to Abby with

Family Ties. She got town council to approve so many things to make the adoption agency possible. Hi, Mayor," she said.

"Good to see *both* of you." Mayor Marsha winked at Luc then patted Holly's shoulder. "Good work with Maxine," she said. "Couldn't have been easy. I could hear her yelling at you from my office."

"Now, Mayor." Holly's cheeks wore an interesting shade of pink. "You know that we never hold anything against a woman who's in labor. It's hard work to have a baby."

Luc gave Holly a lot of credit for that answer. From the look on her face earlier, he'd guessed she'd been irritated by Maxine as she coached the woman through labor, but if so she wasn't willing to put down Maxine publicly.

It was their little secret. He liked sharing it with her. Too bad she wasn't as open with him about why she was always sewing. They couldn't all be baby clothes, could they? Buffalo Gap didn't have that many newborns.

Luc also wondered if she'd opened her dad's trunk yet. He'd hinted six ways through

Sunday that Holly might find something important inside, but she never seemed to take the bait. Marcus had made him promise that when Holly had mourned enough, Luc would get her to look inside. Luc intended to keep his promise.

Now he moved through the crowd, noticing how well he and Holly meshed as they welcomed new arrivals and invited the guests to set up their chairs around the big iron tractor rim he'd placed on bare ground to contain a campfire.

Moments later Mayor Marsha rapped her cane against the table leg to get everyone's attention. After she'd issued strict warnings to the excited children about going too near the fire pit, Luc lit the tinder he'd laid earlier. He'd been worried about having a campfire but as he looked around, he saw that each parent monitored their children.

"Pastor Don's going to say grace for us and then we'll dig into this delicious food," Marsha said. "Thank you for hosting us, Luc."

Luc nodded then edged through the crowd to squeeze in next to Holly. Just before he bowed his head he felt someone's stare. He glanced up and saw Marsha watching him with a knowing smile. In a flush of embarrassment that she'd caught him trying to get close to Holly, Luc bowed his head, listening to the words of gratitude as he savored the pleasure of rubbing shoulders with Holly. She'd been right to encourage him to host this potluck. A sense of overwhelming pleasure flooded him that all these people had come to his home. Maybe soon he'd have a son and host another celebration.

When the grace ended, a line formed at the food table. Luc was relieved to note there were plenty of choices that offered something for everyone. When the children had eaten, Hilda and Henry provided the makings for s'mores. Soon all of the kids and some of the adults were sticky with marshmallows and chocolate.

"Smart idea to put out basins and water pitchers for wash stations throughout the yard," Holly whispered as she passed by. "You're a natural host."

Feeling ten feet tall after such praise, Luc

made sure everyone had what they needed before grabbing his own plate of food. He deliberately sat next to Pastor Don in a spot away from the others because he wanted to pose some questions to the minister.

"I've prayed and prayed but I still don't have a strong feeling about God's plan for me, Pastor," he explained.

"Knowing God's will isn't like putting a quarter into a machine and getting an answer out, Luc." The pastor smiled. "Sometimes we wish it was that simple but the truth is, just getting answers to your prayers isn't enough. The point of prayer is to develop a friendship so you can talk with God. It takes time and patience to understand God, and even more to really hear what He wants to say."

"But I thought God had a plan for my life. Why doesn't He just tell me what it is?" Luc persisted even though he felt slightly foolish for asking.

"Of course He has a plan." Pastor Don nodded. "But that doesn't mean God will dump the complete job description on you like in one of those action movies. I believe that learning our purpose is more of an unfolding that causes us to grow, like a plant that gets rain and sunshine and wind, and slowly matures through all of it."

Luc frowned, not totally clear.

"The way I see it, maybe today God's purpose was for you to host this potluck, which is delicious by the way." Don set aside the bones from his fried chicken and smiled at Luc. "Maybe tomorrow His purpose for you will be something far harder."

"That sounds ominous." Luc frowned.

"It shouldn't," Don said. "The point is to listen and be ready. God never asked you to do great things for Him, Luc. What He asks is for you to allow His greatness to shine through you."

"You're saying that learning God's will isn't necessarily a 'Paul on the road to Damascus moment' that will tell me my future," Luc said, feeling his way. "It's more about being available and communing with God so He can tell me my purpose for today?"

"Yes. It's not always for us to know the big picture but the more we're in tune with God, the more we'll find out His will." Don rose. "Don't get frustrated. Be patient. Talk to God. Let Him speak to you. Read Romans 8, especially verses twenty-six to twenty-eight. Then come and talk to me again."

"Thanks, Pastor." Luc grimaced. "I'm sorry to interrupt your dinner."

"You didn't." Pastor Don chuckled. "Let's go see if there's any of that strawberry pie left. I love strawberry pie."

"We're going to have birth—er, cake, too, so leave some room." Luc moved around the group, picking up discarded plates and cups. He looked for Abby, found her next to Cade, each holding a baby and a bottle. He walked over.

"I guess you're looking for the birthday cake," Abby said in a low voice. "It's in the back of the truck. Want me to help you?"

"No, you're busy. I'll do it. Just make sure you lead us in the singing," he reminded.

"What are you two whispering about?"

Holly appeared at his side, a quizzical look on her face.

"I was going to ask Abby's help with something but she's busy. Care to take her place?" He waited, puzzling out how to do this and still surprise her.

"What do you need?" Holly asked.

"Could you clear a space on the table and have some plates and forks ready? I'm going to get a special dessert I ordered." He watched her face, loving the way she bit her bottom lip to stop from asking him what it was. Luc knew how hard that was for curious Holly.

"No problem," she agreed.

"Now I need— Ooh, there you are." Luc chuckled when Henry suddenly appeared. "Come on, partner."

"But what about the piñata?" Henry asked.

"Okay," Luc agreed sighing inside at the delay. "We can do that first."

Henry dragged Holly with him to watch the kids take turns hitting the rainbow. She cheered as loudly as anyone when it finally spilled candies all over the ground.

Pockets and cheeks bulging, Henry grinned at Luc while Holly and the other ladies helped clean up the remains of the piñata.

"Now we can get the cake," he whispered with a sideways glance at Holly.

"Not that you'll be able to eat any of it after stuffing yourself with that candy," Luc said with a chuckle.

Henry simply grinned.

At the truck, Luc found the cake and took off the lid. A box of candles lay tucked to one side, as the bakery had promised. He let Henry stick all twenty-seven candles in the cake then carried it to the table.

"Happy birthday a day early, Holly," Luc said while Henry drew her forward.

Immediately, Henry burst into the birthday song with Abby's swift support. The guests joined in. Holly stood wide-eyed, trying to smile despite the wetness on her lashes.

"I thought this was supposed to be a community birthday party," she scolded when the song was over.

"It is. But since your birthday's tomorrow,

we wanted to make it a special day for you."
Luc savored her pleasure.

"Blow out the candles," Henry demanded.
"They're melting all over the cake."

"Smart boy," Hilda praised as she patted
Henry's shoulder. "Blow, Holly."

"There are way too many candles," Holly
joked. She puffed up her cheeks so the kids
laughed then blew out all except one candle.

"That means you've got a boyfriend." Henry's grin stretched wide as he called out to
the other kids. "Holly's got a boyfriend."
Then Henry looked directly at her and said
in a voice loud enough for everyone to hear,
"Is it Luc?"

Luc wished he could melt into the dirt of
his ranch as embarrassment turned Holly's
cheeks hot pink. He should have counseled
Henry but it was too late to worry about that
now. He needed to do something to get the
focus off her.

"Of course I'm her friend," he said, swal-
lowing his own embarrassment as everyone
gawked at them. He grabbed a plate and held
it out as Holly cut the cake. "Come on, folks.

Let's see if we can make a dent in Holly's birthday cake."

Thankfully, the group eagerly moved forward. Holly cut large slices that had most of the women groaning and most of the men smacking their lips. When the last guest was served, Luc insisted she enjoy a slice of her cake.

"It was nice of you to do this, Luc." Holly spoke softly so the others wouldn't overhear. "But you didn't have to."

"We all wanted to make your birthday special, even if we are a day early." For some reason he didn't comprehend he didn't want her to know he'd been the instigator. He touched her hand so she would look at him. "I'm sorry if Henry embarrassed you." Her skin felt warm against his.

"It was a nice kind of embarrassment," she murmured before Mayor Marsha called for order.

"Don't worry, folks," Marsha said when someone groaned. "Our only official business tonight is to celebrate Holly's birthday." She chuckled. "So let's visit and enjoy this lovely evening God's given us. A toast to the birthday girl."

There was a loud cheer and a crackly tinkling of plastic glasses. Luc stood in the shadows of the trees savoring the look on Holly's face as folks handed her one gag gift after another. But his biggest pleasure came when he connected the fairy lights and her face lay bathed in their ethereal glow.

Holly paused in reading a card and looked up. She seemed to delight in the delicate glow then lowered her head and scanned his yard, not pausing her search until her gaze met his.

Thank you.

The silent message hit him loud and clear. Luc nodded and mouthed, *You're welcome.*

Someone, probably Henry since he'd helped Luc set things up, started the boom box and soft dreamy music filled the area. Children who had fallen asleep were wrapped in warm quilts and left to rest while their parents danced in a slow rhythm to the dreamy music. Luc wondered who had chosen such romantic music. He jumped a little when he heard a familiar voice in his ear.

"Are you going to dance with me, Luc, on my almost-birthday?" Holly held out her arms, her smile faraway.

"Of course." He slid his arm around her narrow waist and laid his palm against hers before leading her in the mesmerizing beat of the song.

Swaying together as one, they danced under the fairy lights and into the shadows. They danced through friends' laughter and the occasional cry of a fractious child. Luc didn't know how long they danced; he only knew he wanted it to go on forever.

"Did you notice?" Holly's breath feathered over his ear. "They've left and we're all alone." She drew away the length of his arms, her beautiful eyes gleaming. "It was a wonderful birthday evening, Luc. Thank you."

Holly leaned forward and pressed a soft, sweet kiss against his lips. Then she eased from his grip and pointed to a note left on the table that had held the potluck dishes.

Henry's with me. See you. Hilda.

"I'll help you clean up." Holly began gathering leftovers but Luc put his hands on hers.

"No, don't do that."

Holly smiled a funny little smile. "Are you sure?"

He nodded. "I'm sure."

And he was. He was sure that it was time for Holly to go home and past time for him to step back. Being with Holly so much lately had made him emotionally vulnerable. At this moment all Luc wanted to do was keep her in his arms, maybe return that kiss she'd laid on him.

But that wasn't going to happen because he knew too well that fairy tales didn't always end happily ever after and neither did most marriages.

"Go home, Holly. Enjoy tomorrow. You deserve it."

"Oh." She looked confused but eventually turned toward her car. "Okay. Good night Luc," she said, turning back once to say, "Thank you."

"Happy birthday, Holly."

Luc watched until the faint red of her tail-lights disappeared into the night. Then with a sigh of acceptance he unplugged the lights, gathered the remaining debris and poured water over the fire. That was what he needed to do to his strange feelings, because nothing could come of them.

Tomorrow he'd find out Holly's schedule and work out one of his own so he could finish her renovation when she wasn't around.

"You were a lucky man, Marcus," he muttered as he restored the kitchen to its usual neatness. "Holly is a wonderful woman. I'll do my best to help however she needs me, but I won't let her become more than a good friend. I can't."

Chapter Eight

A few days later Holly drove home after a consultation with Abby, preoccupied by the young girl so close to giving birth.

"Petra's afraid of something," Abby had insisted.

"Or someone. The question is who or what?" Holly mused aloud. "So far she's resisted all my efforts to find out. But I'll keep trying."

"I wish she'd realize we only want to help." Abby had waved off Holly's offer to stay, insisting she'd spent far too many hours at Family Ties already.

Now as Holly drove into her yard, she noticed Luc's truck parked under the big poplar tree she and her father had planted on her fifth birthday. For a moment the tree-planting memories marking each year of her life overtook Holly and she paused to let them roll through her mind.

"I miss you, Dad." She took a bracing breath and brushed her fingers across her eyes to erase evidence of her tears.

Odd that Luc was still here. Ever since the night of the potluck he'd avoided her, and Holly was fairly certain she knew why. Because she'd kissed him. If she'd thought twice she wouldn't have done it. But it had been so sweet of him to painstakingly hang those lights just for her.

The town grapevine still buzzed with talk about all the work Luc had gone to in order to make the night before her birthday special. She'd been embarrassed to walk away and leave him with the mess, but he'd been so insistent she go. And truthfully, it had hurt to realize her kiss had left him unmoved.

Not that Holly was looking for anything romantic with Luc, but the way he'd held her, danced with her—it seemed to Holly there'd been something growing between them, something deeper than the casual friendship they'd shared earlier.

"Is something wrong?"

Startled by the voice she'd been imagining, Holly jumped and let out a squeal. "Stop creeping up on me!"

"Really?" Luc lifted one eyebrow then glanced down at his cowboy boots. "Creeping? In these?" He shrugged. "Sorry." He turned and walked toward his truck.

"Luc." Holly had blown it and she knew it. She climbed out of her jeep and hurried toward him. "I'm sorry. It's just that you caught me at a bad moment."

"Oh?" He looked at her with those eyes, and it was like being x-rayed, as if he saw right through her.

"I drove into the yard and noticed that tree." She ignored his dubious look. "I got caught up remembering when Dad and I planted it and, well, I miss him."

"I miss him, too, Holly," he said in a quiet tone. The stern lines that had kept Luc's face impassive a mere moment earlier now dissipated with his soft smile. "Marcus left a big impact on a lot of people."

As you have, Holly thought.

"I was going to tell you that I've about finished with your room." He frowned. "I still have the floor to do but I can't do that with your dad's trunk shoved in the corner. Aren't you ever going to empty it?"

"What is it with you and that trunk?" she asked with asperity. "Can't you just shove it into the dining room or something?"

"I guess." He shoved back his cowboy hat to rub his eyebrow. "But I think you should deal with it. Why keep ignoring it?"

How could she tell him?

"I'm afraid to open it. I don't know what he has in there and…" She couldn't finish, couldn't reveal what was at the root of her hesitation.

"You think he was keeping some secret from you?" Luc frowned again. "That doesn't sound like your dad."

"Yes, it does." She managed a laugh to cover her nervousness. "It sounds exactly like Marcus Janzen to go to great lengths to keep something from his baby girl, especially if he worried it would make her sad."

"I never thought of that." Luc gave her a strange look. Before she could decipher it, he looked away. "What do you think he was hiding?" His voice sounded almost hesitant.

"Something to do with my mother maybe?" It was a relief to finally say it. "I think he always hoped I'd connect with her. It would be like him to feel that was his fatherly duty."

"So what's to be afraid of?" Luc asked.

"I have no desire to try to build some kind of connection after all these years." Exasperated that he didn't understand, Holly blurted, "She gave birth to me but there is no emotional connection. Not like I have with you or Henry."

"Maybe you could build one," he said quietly.

"I don't want to invest myself and be dumped again. Don't you understand?" She was tired of trying to explain how she felt without letting Luc see the bitterness that still festered inside over her mother's treatment of her father. So she turned and strode back to her car.

"Holly, I'm sorry." Luc caught up and grabbed her arm. "It's just that I don't want you to later regret not connecting."

"I won't." He let her go and she removed her purse and a grocery bag from her vehicle. "In all these years she hasn't made any effort to see me. Seeking her out now would be trying to force a connection that neither of us truly wants."

"Then what are you afraid of?" Luc said, his brows drawn together.

"That Dad will have left a note asking me to do just that. I'd have to do it, if he asked," she said.

"So open the trunk." Luc crossed his arms over his chest and stared at her.

"I'll get around to it." Holly walked toward the house leaving Luc standing where he was. When she reached the door, she turned. "Hilda's bringing Henry out for dinner. You're welcome to join us."

"Henry, huh?" He stood there, obviously considering her offer.

"Yes, Henry and steak and blueberry pie," she said curtly, irritated that her presence didn't seem to matter to him. "Dinner's at six. If you're not interested, fine."

Apparently startled by her brusqueness, Luc opened and closed his mouth. Disgusted with his slow response and remembering a time when he would have eagerly sought out her company and her cooking, Holly blew out a sigh of frustration that ruffled her bangs. She went inside. Good thing she'd quashed those silly romantic daydreams because Luc certainly wasn't interested in her.

"And I'm not opening that stupid trunk yet, either, Luc Cramer," she grumbled, shooting the inanimate article a nasty glare as she passed the second bedroom. She'd started toward her room to change clothes when the front door opened.

"I'd like to come for dinner with you and Henry. I'll go do my chores, change and be back by six. Thank you." After that stilted speech, Luc left.

A slow smile crept across her face.

Holly changed and prepared dinner while

puzzling over his attitude. In the past week Luc hadn't sought out her advice and help once. Was that because his adoption plans were proceeding smoothly? That dismaying thought made her pause. Once Luc had permanent custody of Henry, would she be left out?

She was bothered by that thought. She didn't want to relinquish the closeness she and Luc had developed since her father's death. She'd grown accustomed to Luc's protective watch and hated the thought that he would no longer be there for her as he had been.

Perhaps asking him to dinner was a good idea that should be repeated later this week. Or maybe she should change it up with a picnic or a suggestion to accompany Luc and Henry on an outing.

"Inveigling yourself like that is pathetic," she mumbled.

But so was sitting at home sewing baby clothes for someone else when she could be with Luc and Henry. When had her beloved sewing taken such a backseat?

"I'm here," Henry announced, shoving open the door and stepping inside the house. Hilda stood behind him, trying without success to tame his cowlick.

"I didn't even hear you drive up," Holly apologized after hugging the little boy. "It's good of you to bring him out here, Hilda. Would you like to join us for dinner?"

"No, thanks." Hilda preened a little then leaned forward to whisper, "I have a dinner date."

"You look lovely." And she did with that flush of rose coloring her cheeks and anticipation lighting her eyes. "I hope you have a wonderful time," Holly told her.

"I will. Dennis Canterbury is a nice fellow." She smiled at Holly's confused look. "Dennis is the grandfather of that baby girl you delivered this morning."

"Of course. How silly of me to have forgotten." A video of this morning's delivery with friends and family eagerly awaiting the birth of a darling boy with big blue eyes and blond hair played in her memory, creating a block in Holly's throat. "Dennis has a beautiful grandchild," she managed to say around it.

If only she hadn't given her son away, her father would have had a grandchild, too.

"I'd better get going." Hilda patted her freshly set hair. "Do you think this hair color is too bold for a woman of my age?"

"I think you look nice," Henry said, his head tilted to one side as he observed her.

"So do I." Holly slid her arm across Henry's shoulders and smiled at him. "And Henry and I have the best judgment." She winked at the boy.

"Well, I don't know." A faint frown drew lines around Hilda's eyes.

"Don't fuss," Holly ordered. "I'll bring Henry home later and put him to bed at the usual time if you're not home."

"Thank you, dear. You know where the key is." Hilda reached out to smooth Henry's stubborn hair but stopped midreach. She sighed, shook her head and walked to the door.

"Bye," Holly called out at the same time as

Henry. They looked at each other and Hilda and all three of them burst into laughter.

This was what Holly wanted. Friends, family. A person to share her life with. She knew she didn't deserve it, not after what she'd done. That didn't stop the wanting, not that it would do her any good.

"Am I too early?" Luc asked through the screen door.

"Just in time," Holly told him with a smile. Because he always was.

Luc patted Holly's shoulder in his best avuncular manner. Dinner was done and he was looking forward to spending time with Henry and her when she got a phone call. Petra was in labor.

She looked around at the messy kitchen, but Luc preempted her objection.

"Leave the dishes to Henry and me. You go help that girl at Family Ties. She needs you."

"Petra sounded scared." Holly's voice brimmed with worry. "She kept telling me she wasn't due for ages but I knew better. I should have—"

"You can't blame yourself," he said. "You always say babies have their own schedules."

"True." She tucked her phone in her pocket. "What about— Scratch that. I know you can handle anything."

"Almost." Luc grinned.

Holly rolled her eyes. She hugged Henry before striding to the door then at the last minute turned. "I promised Hilda I'd get Henry to bed at her place if she wasn't home by eight thirty."

"Go, Holly," Luc said. "We'll be fine. Take care of Petra. Henry and I will take care of that blueberry pie you made."

"Like I didn't already know that." She hurried out the door. A moment later he heard the roar of her car's motor and the crunch of gravel as she sped away.

"Okay, buddy." Luc ruffled Henry's hair. "It's up to you and me to get this place shipshape for Holly."

"Does shipshape mean cleaning?" Henry asked, his nose wrinkled in repugnance.

"Sure does," Luc assured him with a smile. "Holly made the meal. We clean up. You want to wash the dishes?"

"And get my hands wet?" Henry looked so scandalized Luc burst into laughter.

"Okay, you can dry."

They spent the next few minutes returning the kitchen to its usual immaculate condition. Henry found a domino train game on Holly's shelf. They played until Luc saw Henry's head droop.

"Time to get you back to Ms. Hilda's." Luc smiled when Henry didn't argue.

Hilda was home and waiting for her charge. She sent Henry to prepare for bed then listened to Luc's explanation about Holly.

"So if you can handle it from here, I guess I'll head home," Luc said. "G'night, Henry," he called. Henry came flying downstairs. Luc relaxed into his hug, savoring the precious moment.

Please, God, let him be mine soon.

"I hope that Petra girl isn't playing a game with Holly." Hilda escorted him to the front door. "Something isn't on the up and up with that girl."

"How do you know that?" Luc asked, curious about the comment.

"I've been by Family Ties a few times, Luc. I've heard Petra tell Abby wild, fanciful stories. I've even caught her in a lie myself." Hilda's lips pursed. "Holly's a good girl. She our town treasure. I don't want her hurt."

"You're a town treasure, too, Hilda." Luc hugged her then ducked out the door. "Thanks for watching out for Henry."

"He's a joy," Hilda said. "I'll be sorry when he leaves."

As Luc drove through town he realized Henry had touched more than his own life. Surely God would keep him here, let him be raised among people who really cared about him.

He noticed that the light at the church was on and decided to stop. Andy, the most recent casualty in the marriage department, had called him last night to ask for help and Luc was short on answers. Maybe Pastor Don could help Luc help Andy.

Luc pulled into the lot certain of just one thing. Andy's call had reinforced Luc's certainty that he never wanted to get married. He didn't want to go through what Andy was suffering. He hoped the pastor had some answers for him about God's will. Luc had studied his Bible but still couldn't get a handle on God's plan for his life.

Nor did Luc understand the strange bloom in his affection for Holly. He did know he'd better keep these feelings for her under control because nothing could come of them. He needed to avoid getting too close. Starting a relationship could mean he'd risk ending up as wretched as his friends. No, marriage wasn't for him.

But wasn't it funny that he kept having these thoughts of Holly by his side?

"You're doing well, Petra." Holly smiled at the young girl encouragingly, wishing she'd been able to extract the name of her parents or a friend, anyone who could be here for her. But even after three hours of hard labor, Petra remained adamant. There was no one to call.

"I'm sorry I lied to you." The contraction over, Petra leaned her head against the pillow and inhaled deeply, a sheen of perspiration on her face. "I knew I didn't have long to go but I didn't want anyone poking and prodding at me every day."

"It would have helped us prepare for the birth," Holly said. There was no time for scolding as another contraction gripped the young girl.

"Breathe, Petra. Breathe just as I showed you," Dora Cummings ordered in a no-nonsense voice. "Come on now."

Holly was glad she'd called the nurse to assist. Dora had been invaluable in encouraging Petra to push through the contractions when she would have given up. Ever mindful of the imminent birth, Holly waited until this one was over then quickly checked the girl's progress.

Dora shot a questioning look at Holly.

"It's time," Holly murmured, knowing Dora would understand. "You're doing great,

Petra. When the next one comes we'll ask you to push really hard but when I say stop pushing, you must stop. That's very important. Okay?"

Petra barely had time to nod before a hard contraction grabbed her. Thanks to Dora's support she was able to sustain a push that freed the baby's head. As usual, Holly's heart filled with awe as a fuzzy head appeared. She never tired of the wonders of birth.

"You're doing great, sweetie," Holly praised. "Now one more big push and your baby will be here."

A moment later Petra exerted the final effort and her baby slipped into the world. A tear slid down Holly's cheek as she cradled the little life in her hands. Her breath strangled her when the tiny girl wrapped one small finger around her thumb and clung. Awe exploded inside Holly as the baby's blue eyes gazed at her with sweet innocence.

"Your baby is here," she told Petra. "A beautiful baby girl. You did very well. We'll get her cleaned up and then you can see her."

"A girl." Petra sagged against the pillows

Dora had piled behind her. She showed none of the relief of Holly's usual maternity patients when labor was finally over. In fact, sadness lingered in her gaze. "I don't want to see her. Take her away."

No! Holly wanted to scream it. How could anyone not want this beautiful child? But who was she to judge? With soft, soothing murmurs, she carefully cleaned the baby, weighed her and then swaddled her in a flannel blanket. All the while those big blue eyes studied her. After the first initial cry, the child made no sound. Could she sense that her mother didn't want to hear her voice, didn't want a memory she couldn't delete?

After laying the baby in a small bassinet on the far side of the room behind a screen, Holly finished attending to Petra. She gave her the usual list of instructions after a birth and encouraged the girl to walk, with Dora's help, as soon as she felt able.

But through it all, Holly's attention centered on the infant she'd ushered into this world, a tiny bit of life that would grow into a child, able to love and laugh, to feel joy and sorrow.

The magnitude of what she'd done to a child just like this so long ago swamped Holly in a wave of regret. How could she have given away her own child? How could she now stand by and watch this precious baby be thrust into the world with no one to protect her?

In that instant the idea came to Holly, full-blown, simple, necessary. Maybe, Holly would be able to make up for the child she'd given away. At last she could atone for her sin.

Preoccupied, Holly finished her work at Family Ties. By the time she walked outside into the star-filled night, her every nerve was alive with emotion. She *could* make up for her mistake. She *could* ensure that this tiny, precious life was loved and coaxed to reach her full potential. Surely this was part of God's plan.

"Holly?" Luc's hand rested on her shoulder. "Is everything all right? The baby—"

"—is wonderful," Holly told him. She

took his hand and clasped it between hers, hardly able to stop herself from throwing her arms around him. "Petra had an adorable girl, healthy and strong. Ten on the Apgar at birth and again five minutes later. She's absolutely perfect."

"That's good." Luc leaned back on his heels, a frown creeping across his face. "You look...funny," he said.

"I feel fantastic." Holly let the joy inside her escape in a smile of delight. "I've had the most wonderful idea, something I'm sure you'll support because you're doing the same thing."

"Oh?" He studied her with a worried look.

"I'm going to adopt Petra's baby," Holly told him. "And I want you to help me do it."

Chapter Nine

A week had passed since Holly's stunning announcement that she intended to adopt.

Luc still couldn't process it, couldn't even understand it. That's why he'd made this plan.

I'm going to need some help here, God.

He checked his mental list. A ride, a picnic by a campfire in the hills she loved so well, a beautiful sunset; surely all of those would help her relax. Maybe then he could get her to explain what had led to her momentous decision.

Knowing she'd be home from work by now, Luc rode quickly from his house to hers, barely sparing a moment to admire the beauty of the land now burgeoning with summer beauty. At home, stuck to his fridge was a list of tasks he should be completing. The hay crop was ready to be cut. He needed to cull his and Holly's herds and sell off the cattle they didn't want. There was a yearling in his pasture that needed breaking to halter sooner rather than later.

None of it mattered as much as helping Holly.

"Luc?" Holly stepped out of the house as he rode up, still clad in her work scrubs. It was clear she'd just arrived home because her hair was still bound in the mussed-up ponytail she favored for work. "Is anything wrong?"

"On a day like this?" He told himself to keep it light. "What could be wrong? I came to see if you wanted to take a ride with me to the hills. I need a break."

"Sure. Give me ten minutes." She returned inside her house.

"I'll saddle Melody while I'm waiting." As Luc caught and readied Holly's mare, he mulled over the peculiarities of the week just passed. "First she came up with this crazy idea she was going to adopt. Now she's late every day, her eyes are kind of glassy and all she talks about are babies and what they need."

"Are you talking to yourself, Luc?" Holly stood four feet away, her voice laced with mirth.

"Yes, I am." He handed her the reins. "That way I get the answers I want. Ready?"

"I guess." She swung up into her saddle with a lithe ease that signaled years of riding. "What's wrong?"

"Nothing." He knew she wouldn't let that go. He exhaled. "I'm worried about you."

"Me?" Her blue eyes flared in surprise. "I'm fine."

"Really?" Luc searched for a way to voice his concerns without sounding as if he was trying to interfere.

"What does that mean?" Holly frowned.

"It means you've been different ever since you delivered that baby at Family Ties last week."

"Different? How?" she snapped.

"You came out of Family Ties talking adoption the night Petra's child was born and you haven't ceased since." Luc saw anger building in her eyes and knew he hadn't started well. "I hardly ever hear you mention your sewing lately except to do with that baby."

"What's wrong with that?" Holly's chin jutted out defiantly.

"Nothing, only—" He faltered to a stop, intimidated by her glare. "Adoption?"

"You're adopting Henry." She glared at him.

"It's not the same." But Luc felt hard-pressed to explain why it wasn't.

"The child I want to adopt is female and younger than Henry. Other than that I don't see a difference." Holly reined her horse to a stop then clapped her hands on her hips. "Is this some kind of plan to get me to change my mind?"

"No." Luc saw her skepticism. Holly was so cute when she was steamed. Best not to say that. "Look, I know it's not really my business—"

"No, it isn't." The way Holly's lips pinched together told him he was botching this discussion.

"I just want to understand," he said quietly, infusing every ounce of sincerity he possessed into his voice.

"What's to understand?" Her brows met in a fierce frown.

"Holly, you said you'd never marry." How could he get this frustrating, endearing woman to see reason? "You made no bones about it."

"I'm not getting married, Luc." At least she wasn't chewing him out.

"No, but you also ruled out motherhood. You kept telling me you weren't mother material," he reminded. "Now suddenly you've done a complete reversal. I'm trying to understand why."

"I see." Holly kept staring at him with that narrowed gaze.

"I thought if we could get away for a while, relax and have a picnic supper maybe you'd be willing to explain your plan to me." Luc now had second thoughts about that idea as long seconds dragged by, passed under Holly's intense scrutiny. He held his breath, stifling all the things he wanted to say to her. *Just give me a chance, Holly. Trust me. We're friends. I only want the best for you.* He only exhaled when she finally nodded.

She chuckled as she lifted Melody's reins.

"Next time, Luc, ask me straight out instead of tippy-toeing around." She shot him a prim look then kicked Melody's sides and took off across the green meadow.

"She's mercurial," Luc muttered as he followed. "Is that the word, Lord? Or maybe I mean she's like a puzzle."

Holly rode ahead of him for a long time, letting the wind blow through her hair now that it was free of her ponytail. Luc kept his own pace, figuring she needed time to organize her thoughts. Holly was like that.

When she finally slowed down next to the creek he wasn't surprised. He'd known she'd stop at her favorite place. Luc reined in, tied his horse to a tree and began unpacking while Holly, jeans already rolled up, stepped into the water.

When Luc had his picnic and a small campfire ready, he sat down and watched her, smiling when she dipped her fingers in the water to tease the minnows, chuckling out loud when she slipped and almost splashed face-first in the creek and bursting into loud laughter when a bee chased her.

He didn't think he'd ever get tired of watching Holly. She was interested in everything: a butterfly that landed on a dandelion at the water's edge, a frog that scooted under a stone to avoid her, a robin perched at the water's edge, sipping daintily from the bubbling creek. When she finally came to sit across from him, Luc saw the turmoil in her eyes had settled.

"So what are we having?" She nodded at the cloth he'd spread.

"Ham and cheese sandwiches, chips, iced tea and watermelon." Luc prepared her paper plate, held it out then added his garnish. "With dill pickles, of course."

"Oh, of course," she agreed, her grin charming.

Why was it that Holly's smile always

turned his insides to mush? Luc didn't know and at the moment he didn't care. He was content to simply be with her as the sun moved slowly over the hills. A gossamer breeze whispered across the land, tickling the lush ferns that grew beside the creek. The smell Luc could only describe as summer filled his nostrils. For the first time in many years he felt close to fulfilling his dreams.

So why didn't it seem enough?

He was building his legacy. Soon, hopefully, Henry would live with him permanently. It was what he wanted and yet— Luc crushed that thought to focus on Holly. He understood his goal but what had changed with Holly?

"Look, Luc," she murmured and inclined her head to the right.

A doe and a fawn stepped carefully into the glade on the far side of the creek. The mother deer studied them for several silent moments before she bent her head and began munching on the rich green grass.

Her fawn wandered several feet before it, too, began eating.

"See how she won't let her child out of her sight," Holly said her voice barely audible. "What a wonderful mother she is." There was something wistful in those words.

While Holly gazed at the animals, Luc focused on her. Her head, with its tumble of curls, was tilted just the tiniest bit to one side. A smile tugged at the corner of her lips. Her long arms were clasped around her knees. Luc wondered if she sat like that to contain her fervent joy in life, to keep her from jumping to her feet and rushing toward the animals.

Luc didn't think he'd ever known anyone more lovely inside and out. Holly's beauty made his stomach shiver. He could watch her forever. And that scared him.

"When I delivered Leah the other day, it was like a curtain pulled back and a whole new world spread out before me," she said in a voice so quiet he had to lean closer to hear.

"Leah?" Luc asked.

Holly glanced at him once, smiled then turned her attention back to the doe and fawn.

"Leah is what I call Petra's baby, because she reminds me of Jacob's wife in the Bible, the one he didn't want." She turned her head and made a face at him. "Jacob really loved Rachel but Laban tricked him and made Leah the bride."

"Okay." Luc recalled the story but he didn't understand the parallel.

"Can you imagine how Leah felt?" Holly asked. "The man who loved her sister was willing to marry her in order to get her sister for his wife. How hard it must have been to know she was so unloved, so unwanted."

"But how does this relate to Baby Leah?" Luc asked in confusion.

"Because that's exactly how Petra feels about Leah."

When Holly's eyes welled with tears, Luc's fists clenched. He wanted nothing more than to take her in his arms and comfort her. Instead, he forced himself to remain seated and await her explanation.

"She doesn't want Leah, Luc, doesn't even want to get to know her," Holly continued.

The sorrow and grief lacing her voice swelled the lump in Luc's throat, almost choking him.

"Petra has no idea what she's giving up, let alone how this decision will affect her future," Holly said sadly.

"But you do?" he asked, his curiosity piqued by the way she said that.

"I'm older. I—I can see what she's in for." Holly shot him a quick glance through her lashes.

Not that much older. Luc let it go, eager to hear what had changed.

"I go to Family Ties every day just to hold Leah." Her awe-filled voice dropped. "Every time she lifts her golden lashes and looks at me I feel as if she's begging me to take her home, to give her a family, to want her and love her."

"Holly, I think it's natural that this child draws you in." Luc struggled to find words that would help her. But he was keenly aware that with the lowering sun, the sheltered glade grew increasingly more intimate. "You're a loving person. You helped bring her into this world and you can't bear to think of anyone unloved or uncared for."

"You make me sound like a sickly sweet marshmallow." She stuck out her tongue but the shadows in her eyes remained. "It's more than that."

"Tell me," he murmured.

The way Holly looked now with the glow on her face and her shining eyes forced Luc to realize that what she was feeling lay deeply rooted in her heart. But it also forced him to admit that his feelings toward his amazing neighbor had strengthened to a deep caring he'd never expected to feel when he promised Marcus he'd watch out for Holly. That's what made it imperative that he remain objective, helping to ease her suffering yet still protecting her from any hasty decisions.

"You're frowning. What are you thinking?" Holly asked him.

"I'm remembering the warning you gave me when I told you I wanted to adopt Henry." He paused. "You're kind to want to rescue

Leah, to draw her into your world so you can lavish all the love you have stored up inside." He hated saying this part. "But will the rush of emotions you feel now sustain you through years and years of raising a child on your own, without help?"

"Without *your* help?" She held his gaze.

"Of course I'll help you however I can, Holly," Luc assured her. "Just call and I'll be there. But in the end, you'll be the one responsible for Leah. There would be no going back. You couldn't change your mind."

"I wouldn't want to." Holly didn't blink.

Luc busied himself storing the leftovers from their picnic. He needed a few minutes to process her comments. Her intensity bothered him. It was as if she felt driven to adopt Leah by something more than mere emotion, as if she felt she needed this child to be whole. Was Holly telling him the whole story?

"Leah is part of my heart," she said simply. "How could I tear that out and throw it away?" As soon as the words left her mouth she stopped, gasped and squeezed her eyes closed. A moan escaped through her pinched lips.

"Tell me." Luc reached out and threaded his fingers with hers. "Tell me all of it."

She opened her eyes and stared at him, as if assessing his trustworthiness. Then Holly did a very strange thing. She came to sit right beside him and laid her head on his shoulder.

"Could you just hold me for a minute?" she whispered.

"I can do that." Luc slid his arm around her waist. The contact made his breath catch. A myriad of emotions whistled through him.

On one hand he wanted to draw Holly nearer, hold her closer and try to assuage whatever was bothering her. On the other hand he wanted to vault onto his horse and ride hard toward home, to escape Holly. Why? Because of the strength of his need to hold her, because of the emotions she evoked in him, because of the dreams that having her sit next to him like this engendered. Dreams he well knew he couldn't indulge.

Luc had fought off a similar dream many times this week, knowing how pointless it was to even consider allowing Holly to be that special woman in his life. There couldn't be a future for them. He'd seen over and over that relationships didn't last. They led to hurt and that was the one thing he wanted to spare Holly.

"I don't know how to explain it to you," she whispered after a moment of silence. "From the first moment I held Leah in my arms, it was as if I knew God meant me to have her."

"Because?" he pressed.

"I did something very bad once. Something that ever since I've wished I could change. But I can't." Her voice filled with pain. "I never can. I have to carry that guilt with me."

"Holly—"

"No, let me go on." She inhaled and gave him a watery smile. "Maybe it was the way her eyes locked onto me and wouldn't let go but I could hardly stand to let go of her. When I held her, suddenly my burden of guilt rolled away."

He couldn't stop her, not when her voice grew hushed and reverent. "Go on."

"She made this little mewling sound. Not a real cry. At first I thought maybe her lungs were blocked, but they weren't." Holly's eyes glowed. "She cried when Dora took her, but when I held her again she didn't make a peep."

Luc worried that he wouldn't be able to make Holly see sense, that reality couldn't impede her dream world. But he was being silly. Holly Janzen was the most down-to-earth, practical person he knew. She took everything in stride.

So what was it about this child that had changed her? And what terrible thing had she done? Was that the reason Ron had so abruptly left her?

"Leah is like my second chance. She gives this tiny sigh when I pick her up." Holly gazed at the darkening sky, her mouth lifted in a sweet smile. "As if she knows she's safe with me, that I'll love her forever."

"But you've delivered lots of babies," Luc said. "Why *this* baby?"

"I don't know. I only know that she's given me a new awareness of life." Holly drew a deep breath. "Because of Leah my world has changed."

"How?" he demanded.

"For one thing, I've faced the truth. You were partly right, Luc." Holly smiled at him. "I do want a family. I want children who make me laugh and test me and fill my life."

"So get married. I'm sure half the guys in town would be happy to propose." Luc winced at the thought of Holly marrying any of the local men. None he could name was good enough for her. She deserved someone special.

"I don't want to get married." She shifted against him. "I'm like you. My last relationship really killed my self-esteem. Ron's rejection made it hard to consider a future. I don't think I've ever felt so unwanted in my life."

"I know that feeling," Luc muttered.

"I can't try again, get dumped again and go through the same grueling self-questioning." Holly shook her head. "I'll be left trying to figure out how to get through the rest of my life."

"I doubt that would happen." Luc wouldn't let it. "Not every man is like Ron."

"It's happened to me twice." Holly scowled. "I told you, I don't want to try romance again."

"Got it." Luc closed his eyes and relished these moments with her, knowing they couldn't last.

"But if I did," she said, her voice firm, "bottom of my list would be to get involved with a local guy. Nobody around Buffalo Gap can see past who they *think* I am to the real me. My wonder-girl image just won't go away."

"Holly, no one expects—" She cut him off.

"Face it, Luc, even if they could see that I'm not their 'local girl made good,' if the relationship broke up, I'd be in for another pity party from the entire town." Her face contorted into a mask of horror. "Dumped twice in Buffalo Gap? No way."

"For as long as I've known you, Holly Janzen, you've done your own thing, gone your own way." Luc shook his head in disbelief.

"I can't believe you're worried about what folks in Buffalo Gap think."

She pulled away so she could look him in the eye. As cool air rushed between them an odd sense of loss swamped Luc. He didn't want Holly to distance herself, and yet he felt she was doing that mentally as well as physically.

Daylight had completely faded. Aside from the light given by the moon and the flickering fire, they sat in darkness. The intimacy made Luc doubly aware of how easy it would be to let the feelings that had built up inside spill out. It would be better if they remained unsaid. Imagining a future with Holly had to be suppressed.

"I don't want to get married. I want my own child, Luc." Holly's face lay mere inches from his. Her voice begged for understanding. "You're certain you can raise Henry on your own, aren't you?"

"Yes, but—" He hesitated, uncertain where this would lead.

"If you can raise Henry, why shouldn't I

raise Leah?" she demanded. "Why shouldn't I give that child the love she deserves?"

Holly shifted nearer to the fire, rubbing her hands on her arms to warm them. That simple movement felt like a physical loss. A chill whispered up Luc's spine, but it wasn't only because of the cooler evening air that came between them. It was a gut-deep certainty that something else lay behind Holly's motivation that she kept hidden from him. Something drove Holly that she couldn't or wouldn't explain. All he could offer were words of caution.

"You've never spoken about adopting before. It's quite a surprise that this baby has affected you so deeply," he said. "I wonder if you've thought about this from a different point of view."

"Like what?" Her tone didn't brook meddling.

"A while ago we were talking about God's will. Do you see this as God's plan for you?" He needed her to think this through. "Are you certain that God is directing this and not your heart? Maybe you're trying to fill the hole that Ron left."

Holly stared at him long and hard before she rose, dusted down the legs of her jeans and walked toward her horse.

"Holly?" Luc followed. He touched her arm, not surprised when she flinched. His heart pinched at the sheen of tears that glossed her blue eyes. "I'm not trying to hurt you, Holly."

"You may not be trying to hurt me, but that's exactly what you've done, Luc." Holly fought back the disappointment that felt like a shroud smothering her.

"Please." Luc stood beside her, his face in shadow, his voice pleading.

"No. You listen to me." She would not cry in front of him. "I supported you completely when you said you wanted to adopt Henry. I helped you with Abby, I researched and did the best I could to help you bond with him. I've been there for you, Luc."

"You have. I'm very grateful." His tight voice bugged her.

"Silly me. I thought you'd do the same for me. Because I thought we were friends." She could hardly stomach the thought that Luc opposed her decision to adopt Leah.

"Holly, you're my best friend. I'd never want to hurt you." He hesitated then touched her cheek. "I didn't mean to make you sad."

"Then why—"

"This all came out of left field for me." Luc sighed and raked a hand through his hair. The angle of his stance allowed the moonlight to cascade over his face. He looked so strong, so handsome. So...lovable?

"I've been thinking about it a lot." Holly suppressed her wayward thoughts about Luc Cramer. This was about adopting a baby, not some silly crush on her neighbor.

"You never said anything." He sounded dubious.

"I'm sure I've been talking about Leah nonstop lately, haven't I? She's the best thing in my life right now." As Holly said it, a warm glow filled her. Surely he felt the same about Henry.

"I understand she's special to you." He nodded.

"Then why don't you want me to adopt?" A rush of bitterness boiled up inside her. "You don't think I'd be a good mother?"

"I've told you a hundred times you'd make a fantastic mother, Holly. But you've always said there was no way. Your sudden about-face is confusing. Come, sit down and explain it to me," he invited. "I'll stir up the coals to keep us warm."

"I don't want to talk anymore, Luc." Holly studied his face for a long time. Finally she shook her head. "I've told you my plan. If you can't support me then I'll look to my other friends. But if it's at all possible, I am going to adopt Leah."

She swung up onto Melody's back but kept the mare from moving, bothered by an expression on Luc's face that she couldn't quite decipher.

"Holly, I need to tell you something." Luc's

grave tone caused chill bumps to appear on her arms.

"What is it?"

"I went to visit Petra this week." He held up a hand to stop her comments. "Not to do anything behind your back. I wouldn't do that."

"Then why?" she asked.

"To talk to her. To see Leah. To try and understand your decision," he said very quietly.

"And?" There was more. She could see it in his eyes—something he didn't want to say. "Tell me, Luc."

"Petra doesn't want to keep her baby, but she plans to ask Abby to arrange for a two-parent adoption." The words burst out of him.

It took Holly a moment to comprehend. She reared back as the words struck home. Luc's hand covered hers on the saddle fork.

"Petra was raised by a single mom who never had time for her. When her mother hit tough times, she couldn't handle it, had no one to lean on. She had a severe emotional breakdown that affected Petra badly," Luc explained.

"Petra never told me." Taken aback, Holly sat there stunned.

"She's reluctant to tell anyone." Luc's eyes brimmed with sympathy. "That's why she came here. When her mother learned Petra was pregnant, that there was another mouth to feed, she couldn't take the thought of more responsibility. She's in a mental hospital."

Gutted by his words, Holly sat motionless, trying to digest everything.

"Holly?"

"It doesn't matter," she said, straightening her spine. "Leah is an answer from God for me. He'll work it out." She lifted the reins. "Thank you for the picnic but I'm going home now. I need some time to think. Alone. Good night, Luc."

Holly rode as quickly as she dared toward home, knowing Luc would stay long enough to ensure the fire was completely out. As she rode, she replayed their conversation. Devastation threatened to swamp her.

"You've come through before," she told

herself. "And the way you've made it through is by relying on yourself. You can't depend on anyone except God. You can trust Him."

She could trust Leah, too, Holly decided. A baby wouldn't betray her. Not like Luc had just done. Why hadn't he told Petra what a good mom Holly would make? Why hadn't he stood up for Holly? Why wasn't he there for her?

Because deep down Luc didn't believe Holly should be a mom.

Chapter Ten

How things could change in a few short weeks.

"A few things from Family Ties to welcome her to your family," Holly said with a tremulous smile.

Luc gulped. On the first Monday in July, he stood beside her in front of Family Ties, his heart pounding with fierce pride at Holly's generosity as she laid a gift-wrapped box in the arms of Leah's new parents. He knew the box was filled with the sweet baby garments she'd sewn when she believed Leah would soon be her daughter. With the box transferred, Holly bent and gazed at the child she'd lost.

"Bye, darling Leah."

The words were so quiet Luc might have imagined them except for seeing Holly's lips moving. Her avid gaze riveted on this blessed baby, committing to memory every detail of the child who would never be hers. When she stepped back and waved goodbye to the new family, he knew she was holding back her tears, but her composure wouldn't last long.

That's why Luc was here. That's why he wasn't going anywhere until he was certain Holly was all right, no matter how often she told him she wanted him to leave her alone.

"Can you get me out of here, please?" she asked through gritted teeth, obviously aware of the curious townsfolk watching.

"Let's get coffee at the drive-through then go drink it in the park. I doubt there's anyone using that bench by the river at this hour of the morning." Luc escorted her to his truck and saw her inside. He checked her stoic face once before starting the engine. Silent tears dripped from her chin. "Oh, Holly. I'm so sorry."

"Go, Luc. Please," she begged.

So he bought coffee, handed it to her to hold and headed for the most secluded corner of the town park, made more private by the wide circular hedge which sheltered it from onlookers. A wrought-iron bench sat next to the river. When Holly sat down he handed her a cup then sat beside her. He sipped his brew, waiting for her to open up when she was ready.

"I should have listened to you," Holly murmured, ending the long silence that had fallen between them. "That day up in the hills, I should have listened instead of trying to get my own way. I wish I had. It's just that I thought maybe Leah was some kind of gesture of God's forgiveness. Maybe if I'd listened to you it wouldn't hurt so much now."

"Don't hurt, Holly." He folded her hand in his. Though the morning was hot, her fingers against his were icy. "Think about Leah with her loving parents, safe and secure in a home where she's wanted and celebrated.

God didn't mess up with Leah. He gave her a family to love her."

"I know." Pain lay buried in her voice. "I blamed you, you know. Told myself you didn't have enough faith in me."

"Well, that's wrong." Luc smiled at her. "Because Leah left doesn't mean He's forgotten you or your prayers."

"Why do you say that?" She tossed him a curious sideways glance.

"Because the Bible says that God's plans for us are good and just because there's a delay or a change in course, doesn't mean He's saying no to what we desire. It only means God has something different in mind."

"It wasn't long ago you were questioning God's will," Holly remarked in surprise.

"I guess I'm learning to trust." Luc desperately wanted to help this tender, giving woman get past her grief and see the potential in her world. "You have so much to give, Holly."

"I don't want to give anymore." She lifted

her gaze to meet his. "I want my own way. I want Leah."

"I know." He squeezed her fingers, loving her honesty. Instead of diminishing after the campfire a week ago, his emotional bond with Holly had strengthened. Her sadness was his because she was an integral part of his world.

"When will losing Leah stop hurting, Luc?"

"Maybe when you get involved with others." He grinned. "In that vein, I wouldn't say no if you wanted to help me today."

"With what?" She studied him so curiously Luc could only hope this idea worked out.

"I promised Henry that the day camp he's attending this week could come out to the ranch this afternoon." Luc faked a shudder. "I could really use some help."

"Don't play me, Luc," Holly said with some asperity. "You're trying to cheer me up by giving me a job but I know you're perfectly capable of entertaining those kids."

"I'm not—" The look she shot his way made him pause.

"As it happens I am at loose ends today and

keeping busy with a bunch of kids is exactly what I need to wear me out." Her backbone straightened. "When do they arrive?"

"Half an hour. They'll stay for lunch," he told her deadpan.

"What?" For a second lovely Holly Janzen's mouth dropped. Then she regained control, capped the lid on her coffee and rose. "Well, let's get out there. Why are you dallying here with me?"

"I like dallying with you." He doubted she knew how true that was.

"Luc." Holly walked with him to his truck then laid her hand on his wrist. "I'm sorry about—"

"No. I'm sorry." He tapped a gentle forefinger against her lips. "But the thing is, friends don't need to apologize to friends." He lifted his hand away. It was either that or smooth his fingers over her cheeks, slide them into her hair and press her head to his shoulder.

"Friends shouldn't be such jerks when other friends are only trying to help them." She held his gaze. "Should they?"

"Nope." He grinned at her.

"I should never have expected to adopt Leah," she admitted. She stared at her feet. "I should admit that when I was trying to pray about it, I knew I was really asking for my own way and not God's will. I don't deserve Leah."

"What do you mean?" Luc frowned.

"Not getting to keep Leah, that's God's punishment," Holly murmured.

"God isn't like that." Luc couldn't fathom anything Holly could do that would bring God's punishment. "God is love," he said firmly. And how could God help but love sweet, tender Holly?

"We should go. Your guests will be arriving." Holly forced a smile that didn't reach her eyes. "I'll get my jeep, drive myself and meet you there. Do you need any supplies?"

"No. I have everything I need." But as Luc watched her walk away, he knew it wasn't true. He needed Holly. But he knew he would fail at romance.

But I can be her friend. I can help her

heal, find new possibilities, new ways to give from that loving heart of hers.

Luc's dreams of the future always included Holly. She would be an essential part of his future with Henry. She was the first one Luc thought of whenever a problem stymied him. Now Holly's happiness was becoming the most important thing in his world.

Is that love?

"I want her to be happy," he prayed as he drove to his ranch. "But that isn't love. It can't be."

Because falling for Holly would mean opening himself up for rejection and the one thing Luc did not want to experience with Holly was rejection.

"I'll be her best friend, God," he promised.

Somehow that felt like second-best.

"Thank you for asking me to help, Luc," Holly panted, opting out of the rousing game of dodge ball to stand by him. "This is exactly what I needed."

"We're certainly glad you came, Holly." Local teacher Georgette Finstead had again volunteered to lead Buffalo Gap's one-week summer day camp for local kids. "This class is the biggest our program has ever had. I'll take all the hands I can get. Luc's been wonderful to let us come out here."

Holly barely covered her snort of disgust as the teacher simpered at Luc who backed away as if he'd been stung. He shot Holly a look of pleading.

"If you can manage alone for a few minutes, Luc and I could sure use a break," she said to Georgette. "We ranchers get up before the sun."

"Oh, by all means." Georgette turned to correct some misbehavior, and Holly yanked on Luc's arm.

"Stop staring at her hair," she hissed.

"I can't help it," Luc muttered. "How does she get it to stay piled on her head like that?"

"I wouldn't know," Holly mumbled, feeling disheveled and sweaty beside the pristine Georgette. In the shade of a poplar tree, she poured them each a glass of lemonade and handed one to him, which he swallowed in one gulp.

"I only wondered because the wind's been strong all afternoon but her hair hasn't moved a bit." Luc shrugged. "Weird."

Why should she feel relieved that he wasn't interested in the lovely Georgette? Holly wondered. Luc was a good man and even if he didn't want a romantic relationship, he deserved to find happiness.

Only not with Georgette.

"Did you say something, Holly?" Luc asked her.

Could he hear her thoughts? "Just that your truck looks good," she said quickly. "Is the restoration finished?"

"Not quite." His grin stretched from one ear to the other. "But rest assured I'll have it ready for the parade next month. My fingers are itching to claim that five-hundred-dollar prize."

"Mine, too." When he stared at her she reminded, "For the biggest pumpkin."

"Oh. Right." He grabbed one of the gingersnaps she'd brought and sampled it. "These are the best. When did you have time to bake?"

"Last night." She gulped and forced herself to continue. "When I still hoped maybe I'd be celebrating Leah's arrival."

"Well, it was nice of you to bring them." He popped the rest of the cookie in his mouth. "Do you think the kids had fun?"

"They had a blast," Holly assured them. "Hiring Sadie Smith as the clown was perfect. Her magic show gave them a break between games." She put her hands on her hips, leaned back and studied him. "Are you sure you haven't tried parenting before?"

"That's the best compliment you could give me." Luc grinned and suddenly Holly's heart danced light and carefree. "At least no one's complained about the mosquitoes," he said, slapping at one buzzing near his head.

"They're too busy having fun to notice the odd bug." She plucked her T-shirt away from her body. "I am going to appreciate a cool shower after this."

"Not me. I'm riding up to the creek." Luc grinned. "Want to come?"

"Oh." She closed her eyes and imagined

that cool water covering her. "Yes, I do. I think this is the hottest day we've had so far this year. Swimming will be fantastic at the creek."

It was only when Georgette cleared her throat that Holly realized she and Luc had been staring at each other for a long time.

"As you see, we're getting ready to load the bus and return to town, but the children want to thank you, Luc." Georgette linked her hand through his arm, her doe eyes fawning. "As do I. It's been a wonderful afternoon."

"My pleasure." Luc tried to ease his arm free, but Georgette wasn't letting go, so he winked at Holly and caught her hand in his other arm. "Thank Holly also. I couldn't have done it without her help."

Holly chided herself for the smug satisfaction she found in Georgette's grimace. How could she have doubted Luc's friendship?

"It's to be expected Holly would help make this afternoon a success. After all, she's the town's goodwill ambassador. So thank you, Holly," the teacher said.

It should have been a compliment but in Holly's eyes it was just another expectation people placed on her.

"No thanks needed, Georgette." Holly eased away from Luc, unsettled by the reaction his touch brought. She liked Luc holding her arm a little too much. She waited until the kids had performed their goodbye song then found Henry and gave him a hug. "Did you have fun, honey?"

"Tons," he said between chewing the last piece of watermelon. "Only I wish I could have showed the kids my room here."

"Maybe next year, when you start first grade," she said, ruffling his hair.

"Yeah. When me an' Luc are a family. And you'll be here, too, Holly." Henry grinned then gave her a sticky hug. "See ya, Holly."

"See you, sweetie." She stood and waved away the busload of children while thinking about Henry's comment. She'd be here, too, he'd said. But would she? Where did she go from here? What did God want for her?

"It seems so quiet," Luc said from behind her. "Not that I'm complaining. That was a whole lot of kids at one time." He flung an arm across her shoulders and led her back to the party remains. "You're not leaving me with the mess this time."

Holly marveled at the wealth of odd feelings whirring inside her. She felt light, almost carefree after such a difficult start to her day. But when Luc removed his arm, some of her pleasure evaporated. Why?

"Do you have to work tomorrow?" Luc began clearing off the table where they'd served a snack.

"Two whole days off. Why?" she asked.

"Because I don't want to come back from the creek until I'm good and cooled off." His gaze narrowed. "I'm going to be late."

Holly stared at him, knowing that with Luc's help she could get through the hovering sense of dejection waiting to engulf her. She'd keep seeking God's will even though the cloud of guilt lingered. Luc would help her. He wouldn't let her down.

Holly grabbed the end of the paper tablecloth and rolled it toward him, bundling the whole thing into his arms. Luc had been there for her this morning when she thought she'd betray herself to Leah's parents. He'd supported, encouraged and helped her all these months since her dad's death. Maybe, just for a little while, she'd depend on him.

"What I'm saying is that I don't intend to rush home." Fun danced in his dark eyes. He was so good-looking. "Any objections?"

"Nope. No objections at all," she said and meant it.

"Well, glory be. Miss Holly Janzen is going to let loose in the creek," Luc teased.

"You know," Holly said slowly. "I think I just might." *But only with you, Luc.*

"Watch this!" Holly ordered.

Luc was pleased to do so. She looked so lovely with the sun glossing her wet hair as she danced from rock to rock across the creek, her cutoff shorts revealing her tanned limber legs.

"You'll slip," he warned then caught his

breath when she did. He half rose to go rescue her but she recovered her balance, twisted her head and winked at him. "Show-off."

"Of course," she said in a dry tone, flopping down beside him. "After all I was voted Buffalo Gap's girl most likely to do everything, achieve anything and generally become a role model to emulate," she said with a wink.

"And you have." Luc handed her a soda from the cooler he'd brought along. "Haven't you?"

"No." She leaned back and let the sun take away the chill of the water.

"But you're very successful in your work." He saw the way she shifted uncomfortably and wondered what was bothering her. "Abby told me you were offered a very nice position in Calgary's biggest hospital this morning."

"Which I promptly declined." Holly shrugged. "Not that they accepted that. They've given me a month to 'think it over.' As if I need to."

"There's no upside to that job?" Luc asked.

"Not enough. I like knowing my clients, watching the babies I deliver grow up. I like living in Buffalo Gap and I love being involved in Family Ties." A sad look flitted across her face before she chased it away and grinned at him. "So don't go thinking you're going to buy Cool Springs Ranch anytime soon 'cause I'm not selling."

"Duly noted." Luc nodded. "So what are your hopes and dreams for the future, if that's not being too nosey?" He saw the way she caught her breath then tried to cover her discomposure.

"At the moment I don't have any." Holly spread her arms wide. "I'm going to relax, enjoy the summer and wait for God to show me what's next."

"Not a bad idea," he said with a nod. "Anytime you want to talk, remember I'm just a call away."

"Thanks, Luc, but what about you? We're always talking about me," she said in a guilty tone. "What's happening with you and Henry?"

"As far as I know, everything is progressing well," he told her. "One of these days I'm going to take him to see his brother."

"In prison?" Holly sounded surprised.

"Yes. Henry keeps saying how much he misses Finn." He frowned. "I want to adopt Henry but that doesn't mean I want to exclude the only family he has."

"Good for you," she praised, looking slightly stunned.

"His parents are dead. Finn's all the family he remembers." Luc turned to study Holly. No matter where or when he saw her, she always looked lovely. "Want to come with us?"

"I'd love to. Just tell me when." She nodded then narrowed her gaze. "But you seem preoccupied with something. If not Henry then what?"

Luc hesitated. It was one thing to try to help your buddies. It was something else entirely to share their personal problems with someone. But he trusted Holly and she had good instincts about people. Maybe she could give him some ideas of how to help his friends.

"Luc?" She laid her hand on his, a concerned look darkening her eyes.

"Remember I told you my friend is getting a divorce?" When she nodded, he turned his palm so his fingers could mesh with hers. "Actually it's not only Pete, it's three of the most devoted men I've known trying to work through marriage breakdowns. I've tried but I don't feel like I'm helping."

"Maybe it's not up to you to help," she said after several moments' pause.

"But I'm the one they turned to," he spluttered.

"I know. You've been a great friend and spent hours letting them speak their hearts. You must have spent time searching for godly ways to advise them." She smiled. "I'm guessing they've exhausted your suggestions?"

Luc nodded, curious as to where this was leading.

"What's the next step?" Holly's fingers tightened on his.

"I'm out of suggestions. All I can say is keep trying, for the sake of their family." He hated that. How could relationships as intense as his buddies' had been just be over?

"Maybe it's time for them to let go." At her words, he jerked forward. Holly held up one hand. "Don't shoot me down yet, Luc."

"But what you're saying is unacceptable," he insisted.

"Is it?" She squeezed the hand he still held then drew away. "Or is it the failure of their marriages that is unacceptable?"

"I— I—" He couldn't find the right words.

"You're a good man, Luc. When you make a commitment, you make it for life. That's the way it should be," she said. "But life doesn't always turn out that way."

"You're saying I should tell them to walk away?" He couldn't wrap his mind around that.

"No, I'm saying that maybe it's time to step back and assess." He could tell she'd given the subject some thought. "These men—their situations are sad and hurtful but unless their wives change, there's not really any way to revive their marriages, true?"

Luc nodded, hating to admit what was clearly true.

"So perhaps it's time to think about how to manage this new dynamic so they keep close to their children. Maybe it's time to let go and wait for God to show them a new path for their lives. That's what I'm going to do." Holly jumped to her feet and beckoned him. "Time for another swim."

"You go. I'm still shivering from the last one." Luc watched as Holly raced to the edge of the creek and then slid down into the frigid water with a choked-off scream.

Let go and wait for God to show them a new path. Not bad advice and equally applicable to his own life.

Luc's heart thudded with pleasure as he watched her float down the creek, eyes closed, face tilted upward. Holly was part of his world, part of his life. A day without Holly in it was empty. The next few weeks without Leah would be rough for her, but he'd be there.

He'd always be there for Holly. But that wasn't love. That was pure friendship.

Somehow Luc would need to be content with that.

Chapter Eleven

"Come on in, Luc. Help yourself to iced tea. I'll finish this seam and I'll be ready to leave."

At his agreement Holly started her machine and zipped down the seam, glad for the air conditioning that made the late July heat bearable. With a sigh of relief she laid the receiving blanket across her new work surface and paused a moment to admire her embroidery work.

"I'm finished." She glanced over one shoulder to smile at him. "Hi."

"You never told me why you're always sewing baby clothes." Luc's gaze locked on the small pink, blue and green striped boxes stacked on top of her father's chest. "Those can't all be for friends' babies."

"They're not." She swiveled in her chair to face him and decided it was truth time. "I'm running an online business, Luc. I sell baby clothes made to order. I needed a way to pay off all those things I bought to make Dad's last days easier."

"But couldn't you have sold that stuff and recouped some of the money?" He scratched his head. "Instead, you donated everything."

"Because somebody else might need them and not be able to pay for them." She shrugged. "Anyway, I like sewing."

"You must if those are all orders you've filled." Luc looked without success for a place to sit. "How come nobody in town knows?"

"Because I've taken special pains to keep it quiet. I go to the next town to mail the packages. I have a mailbox there, too, just to make sure nobody finds out when I pick up the supplies I order online." She couldn't avoid his stare.

"Why go to such lengths?" Luc said.

"The truth?" She chided herself for not trusting him.

Luc nodded, leaned against the door frame and waited.

"After the thing with Ron, everybody in town felt sorry for me. It was horrible. Then I couldn't have Leah. If they also knew I was making baby clothes, can you imagine what they'd say?" She shuddered. "'Poor Holly. No marriage, no children so she consoles herself making baby clothes.' No way do I want that."

"Did anyone ever tell you that you worry too much about what other people think?" Luc shook his head. "What is it with you and this hang-up about being the town's good girl? Nobody's watching you to see if you mess up, Holly."

"Aren't they?" She cringed at the memory of the discussion she'd overheard at Maxine's baby shower. *Holly, these outfits are so cute. When are you going to have your own kids to sew for?*

"Are they?" He frowned. "I haven't heard anything."

"Sure you have. Georgette hinted as much." When he didn't remember she repeated, "'Holly's the town's goodwill ambassador.'"

"Isn't that a good thing?" he asked.

Luc didn't get it. Well, how could he? He was a relative newcomer to the area and Holly knew that to clarify would make her sound like a whiner. For reasons she couldn't explain to herself right now, she didn't want Luc to see her in such a negative way.

"I'm ready to go if you are," she said as she rose. "I gather we're picking Henry up as we go through town. Is he excited about seeing his brother?"

"I'm not sure." Luc followed her out of her house, waited while she locked the door then walked beside her to his truck. "I tried to explain everything that would happen but he hasn't said much. Hilda says he hasn't talked to her, either. I'm thinking he probably hasn't processed everything yet."

"Or maybe he's afraid of going to the

prison," Holly suggested as they bumped down the gravel road that led to town.

"Maybe. We'll just have to help him through. Okay, partner?" he asked, grinning.

"Deal." How she liked that word, *partner.*

Henry was indeed subdued when they found him sitting on the front stoop with Hilda. He told her goodbye then with Luc's help, climbed into the truck to sit beside Holly.

"How are you, Henry?" Holly asked, slightly worried by his solemn look.

"Okay, I guess." His hand slid along the seat and curled it into hers.

"I bet you're excited to see Finn. It's been a while, hasn't it?" Her worries mushroomed at his monosyllabic response. "Honey, what's wrong? Luc and I will be there the whole time. You don't have to be scared."

"What if Finn doesn't want me to be 'dopted?" Henry finally said. "He's my brother."

"It doesn't matter what happens, Henry," Luc said. "Finn will always be your brother.

That's never going to change. Brothers are forever."

"Oh." The boy's brow cleared immediately. His eyes began to glow with excitement. "Could Finn come to the ranch sometime and see my bedroom? And I'd show him the horses and the tire swing that you made for me and the place where I feed the cows."

Holly looked over his head at Luc, with a what-do-we-do expression.

His smile charmed her, before he looked at the boy. "You know, Henry, I think you and Finn should discuss that. You could tell him that you'll write him a letter and he can write you back and let you know if he wants to come for a visit."

"I'll be in first grade soon," Henry said thoughtfully. "I'll be able to write really good, won't I?" Once they'd assured him, Henry borrowed Holly's iPod and settled down to listen to music she'd recorded for him.

"That's very generous of you to have Finn," Holly said, impressed by Luc's settling of Henry's fears.

"Family is always family. Henry and Finn should remain close," he said.

How generous Luc was. He was accepting Henry lock, stock and convicted felon brother. Which was as it should be, of course. It was just that Holly didn't know many men who'd insist on retaining a familial connection like that. Luc's determination to embrace Henry unconditionally sent her esteem of him even higher.

With the radio quietly playing in the background, Holly got lost in her thoughts about the man she called her best friend. Lately Luc stopped by for coffee a lot if she was off work. They'd gone twice more to the creek for a swim. She'd helped him arrange a treasure hunt for Henry on the ranch and the three of them had worked together to clean his restored vehicle and prepare it for the upcoming parade.

What Holly hadn't done, despite Luc's repeated reminders, was open the trunk her father had left. She'd finally realized her father had tasked Luc with getting her to look in the trunk. And she would. One of these days when it didn't hurt quite so much to see it and remember all the stories her dad had told her about the trunk's travels with him through Africa where he'd bought it.

"Are you asleep, Holly?" Humor threaded Luc's voice. When she looked at him, he smiled. "We're here."

Holly wasn't sure what to expect. All she knew was that she had to keep a close eye on Henry and soothe his fears. So when they entered the prison she held on to his hand, even though she knew he thought he was too old to need such attention.

The three of them were shown into a small room where they waited for only a few minutes before a young man entered.

"Finn!" Henry tore his hand free, raced across the room and threw himself into his brother's arms.

"Hey, Henry." Finn, an older version of Henry, gathered the boy close, closed his eyes and savored the joy of holding his brother. "Long time no see, buddy." Pure joy radiated across his thin face. His eyes, mirrors of Henry's, took in every detail.

"Your hair is different. It looks good. Are you behaving?"

"Uh-huh." Henry grinned. "This is Luc and this is Holly. They're my friends."

"Nice to meet you, Finn. Luc Cramer." Luc held out his hand, waiting until Finn finally extended his and shook it. "I've heard a lot about you from Henry. He says you like to work with wood."

"Yeah." Some of the hesitancy vanished from Finn's face. He dug in his pocket and pulled out a small animal. "I heard you were staying on a ranch so I made you this horse, Henry."

"Thanks." Henry grinned adoringly at his big brother then reverently took the horse from Finn's hand. "You made it look just like Holly's horse. He's called Babycakes."

"For real?" Finn asked wide-eyed.

"For real. I'm Holly Janzen." She shook Finn's hand. "Luc and I are ranching neighbors but Henry lives with Ms. Hilda." She knew Finn was almost eighteen but was surprised by how young he looked. "I'm glad to meet you. A brother of Henry's has to be very special."

"Thanks." Finn gave her an embarrassed smile then his attention returned to Luc. "I was told you want to adopt my brother." He watched Henry gallop his horse around the room.

"Yes, I do. I want to give him a home. Henry's a very special boy and I love him dearly," Luc said quietly.

"So do I." Finn's look challenged Luc, but Luc didn't take the bait.

"I know you do, Finn." He didn't retreat from the confrontation in the brother's eyes but kept his tone friendly. "Henry's told me all about how you looked after him. You did a great job of raising him."

"He's a good kid," Finn muttered.

"Due to your influence," Luc agreed. "I hope when you get out you'll come and see us at the ranch. Henry talks about that a lot."

Holly's heart melted at Luc's gentle tone as he tried to reassure this big brother that he had no intentions of cutting him out of Henry's life. It was a brilliant way to ensure

Henry's adjustment to Luc was made even easier. Luc's big heart was as large as his ranch, Holly thought fondly. He made her world and Henry's and Finn's a better place. How she loved him for it.

Wait a minute. *Loved* him? That couldn't be.

"Right, Holly?"

"Huh?" She blinked, found Luc frowning at her.

"What's wrong?" he asked.

"Nothing." She blushed at Finn and Henry's curious stares. "Just thinking."

"I was telling Finn that if he wants to look for a job near Buffalo Gap there's always someone hiring." Luc gave her a funny look.

"That's true," Holly agreed, trying not to show that Luc's proximity had such a strong effect on her. "If that's what you want. What are your interests, Finn?"

Finn spoke of his love of carving. Moments later he and Luc were bent head to head discussing wood.

"I'll find out if I can send you some hickory," Luc promised when the guard told them the visit was over. "I've heard that it's great for carving."

"Thanks a lot." Finn shook his hand, his face now relaxed. "And thanks for caring about Henry. I appreciate it."

"It's entirely my pleasure," Luc assured him.

"I don't want to go." Henry leaned against Finn's leg as he gazed at his brother. "I don't want to leave you here. I missed you, Finn."

"I missed you, too, Henry." Finn lifted the boy on his knee and reminded him of some of the fun things they'd shared. They laughed together, each adoring the other. "I'm sorry I messed up, Henry. I did a bad thing by stealing. I shouldn't have done it. That's why you had to go live with someone else. Because I made a mistake."

"Luc says everybody makes mistakes," Henry said, cupping his hand against Finn's cheek. "You have to ask God to forgive you," he said earnestly.

"I already have," Finn told him quietly. "And I know He heard me because He sent you to some very nice people. God sure does care about you, Henry."

"He cares about you, too," Henry said a little tearfully.

"When I get out of here I'll come and see you," Finn promised, holding the boy tightly. "Maybe I'll even try sitting on one of Luc's horses."

"Really?" Henry asked. Hope filled his face, and Holly's heart squeezed tight. "You won't do anything bad again? I know I made you do it."

"No, Henry." Finn's stern voice surprised the boy. He shifted but Finn hung on to his shoulders and waited until Henry looked at him. "Nothing that happened to me was your fault, Henry. Understand? *I* did something wrong and now I have to pay for it."

"But I told you the teacher said I needed new glasses," Henry said, his voice brimming with contrition. "If I hadn't told you—"

"Wasn't I old enough to know not to steal?" Finn shook his head. "You didn't do anything wrong, Henry."

"Sure?" Henry saw Finn's nod but apparently that wasn't enough. He looked to Luc who also nodded then to Holly who did the same. "Okay," he said at last with a big sigh.

"We have to go now, Henry," Luc said quietly. "But we can come back another time. If you want to."

"I want to," Henry said, his chest thrust out proudly. "Finn's my brother. We hafta stick together."

"Exactly the way it should be." Luc said goodbye to Finn, waited for Holly to do the same then ushered her outside the room, giving Finn a moment with his brother.

"That kid is one of the good guys," he said, his voice thick with emotion. "I'm going to ask Abby to do some investigation and see if the court will grant Finn early release if he's under my supervision."

What a guy. Holly could no more have stopped herself from throwing her arms around Luc and pressing a kiss against his cheek than she could have stopped breathing. When she stepped back, Luc blinked at her as if he'd survived a whirlwind.

"What was that for?"

"For being a wonderful, caring, generous, sweet man," she said.

"Sweet?" His nose wrinkled.

"Yes." She linked her fingers with his. "Do you know how much I admire you, Luc Cramer?"

"They're just kids trying to raise each other," he said, brushing off her compliment. But he didn't let go of her hand. "I want them to be together."

"You deserve to be a father," she whispered as Henry came out of the room.

Together they walked to Luc's truck. Then he drove them to an ice cream stand and bought the biggest cones they offered. As they sat in the hot sun licking their ice cream, Holly offered a silent prayer.

Lord, I do love this man. I love him more than I ever dreamed I could love Ron, miles beyond the love I thought I had for my baby's father. Luc stands head and shoulders above every man I've known except Dad.

But how could an honest, decent man like Luc care for the real Holly Janzen? Not the local girl everyone thought always did the right thing, but the girl behind the mask, the one who'd given away a child she'd carried for nine months right next to her heart because she didn't want anyone to know she wasn't the shining example they thought?

Holly wasn't worthy of Luc. A man like him, gentle, sincere, trusting—how could he possibly understand what she'd done? Luc deserved the best life had to offer. The best was not Holly Janzen, though she dearly wished it was.

Chapter Twelve

"I've only ever ridden in a parade before on my horse." Holly waved at bystanders as Luc drove the route. "It's more fun riding in your truck, especially knowing you won first place."

"Don't forget I also took first place for the best historic entry with this baby," Luc bragged, patting the steering wheel. "But I couldn't have done either without you and Henry to help." He glanced over his shoulder and grinned. "Okay back there, Henry?"

"Yes." That was all Henry had said since the moment Luc had lifted him into the restored truck. Dressed in a Western shirt Holly had made for him, jeans and the cowboy boots Luc had provided, he clung wide-eyed to a black Stetson, smaller but identical to Luc's.

The band behind them struck up another number so talking was, for the moment, impossible. That was okay with Luc. He couldn't put what he was feeling into words anyway. Or maybe he could. One word. Perfection.

These past weeks he, Holly and Henry had done everything together from creek-side picnics, hay rides with Henry to just generally enjoying God's creation. Studying his Bible seemed so much easier now that he'd laid off trying to instruct his buddies and instead met with them one evening a week to talk about God and pray. Every day Luc felt he learned a little more about the Father to Whom he'd given his life.

He'd also given up, at least for now, trying to figure out the master plan for his life. Instead, he'd settled in to taking one day at a time, doing the best he could and waiting for God to show him the next step. Most of those steps he'd taken with Holly at his side.

She fit perfectly in his world and Luc could not imagine life without her sweet smile and charming laugh.

This summer had been the best of Luc's life. That was because of Holly. She made every day such fun that the days she couldn't join him and Henry to play seemed dull and long. Luc had finally accepted that he was falling for his boss.

And yet he was bothered by the fear of being emotionally tied, even to a wonderful woman like Holly whom he trusted more than anyone. A part of him feared his soul-deep longing for her because lately he'd begun to wonder if he knew the real her, the one she said no one ever saw.

Since Leah's departure, Holly had grown less jovial, more introspective, or perhaps the word was *contemplative*. At first Luc thought she'd finally opened her father's chest and that something in it troubled her. But he'd seen that chest sitting in her sewing room just this morning, still locked tight. So it wasn't that.

What if she isn't who I think she is, Lord?

"Be still and know that I am God." The verse from Psalms filled his head, chasing away the doubts for a moment.

But then Luc saw the way she gazed with longing at an infant in its mother's arms, and his concerns came rushing back. What if he took the risk, told her of his feelings and Holly didn't reciprocate? Worse, what if something later came between them?

Was a relationship with Holly God's will?

"We turn off here, Luc." Holly drew him from his introspection by touching his arm.

Luc nodded and made the turn as he made his decision. He wasn't going to say anything yet. Not until he'd totally thought this through. He'd stick with the status quo. For now.

"You're parking here?" Holly arched her eyebrows as she glanced around the empty field next to the fairgrounds. "We'll have to walk forever to get to the exhibits," she complained.

"Should I drop you there?" He flushed when she stared at him. "I don't want any-

one to ding my door if they park too close,"
he confessed. "I just refinished it."

"Well, Henry." Holly grinned at the boy.
"Guess we're taking a walk."

"Can I put my own shoes on?" Henry asked
plaintively. "These boots hurt my feet."

Luc helped Henry change shoes, then they
walked hand in hand to see if Holly's pumpkin had won a prize.

"It's ginormous," Henry whispered, gaz-
ing at the massive orange pumpkin.

"But it doesn't have a blue ribbon," Holly
said, sounding a bit let down.

"It has a red one. You won second place
and two hundred fifty dollars," Luc told her.
"That's not bad for a first timer. Let's go see
how your quilt did."

Holly held back a little, and Luc knew why.
She didn't want to see that the quilt she'd
crafted specially for Leah had received second place, or worse, no award at all. Holly
was still emotionally bound to Leah.

"Be positive." He took her hand and led
her to the area where quilts of all sizes and
colors hung across the hall. "Look, Holly."

Holly's quilt lay spread against a section of the brown paneled wall where its delicate pink, blue, gray and yellow blocks joined together to become a meadow where wildflowers bloomed around a child.

"It's so pretty," Henry said. "Like a picture."

"A very beautiful picture," Luc agreed. He drew her forward to study the tag. "And it's taken first prize with a recommendation to be entered in the national quilt show in Vancouver this November. Congratulations, Holly."

Amazing work, incredible craftsmanship. One of a kind. As Holly read the words on the tag the judges had affixed, a tear tumbled down her cheek.

"Aren't you happy?" Henry asked, his face puzzled.

"People are going to see this beautiful quilt and applaud the talented woman who created it." Luc threw an arm across her shoulders and squeezed.

"No, they're not." Holly swiped away her tear and smiled at him. "This quilt isn't going anywhere except into a box for my friend Dora. She just found out she's pregnant."

Which was nice, but also meant that if Holly gave the quilt away she wouldn't have to look at it anymore and be reminded of Leah. Luc's heart melted.

Please, God, Holly's such a special woman. She deserves to be happy. Please help me bring some joy into her life.

From that moment Luc devoted himself to making it a day to remember. He insisted Holly help him persuade Henry to try every ride in the children's area, especially the miniature ponies. He paid for Holly to try her hand at a water gun gallery, but when she lost, Luc took over and won a huge teddy bear. They both cheered when Henry won a rubber duck.

They sampled burgers and fries and hot dogs and Luc fed Holly onion rings. They stopped by the local Rotary booth for a piece of homemade pie. They watched chuck wagon and chariot races. Luc couldn't stop laughing when Holly's abysmal choices continually came in last.

And finally, with the sun sinking into the western sky, Luc sat with his arms around Holly and Henry as they rode the Ferris wheel. And that's when he knew for sure that this was what he really wanted. A woman, Holly, to love and to cherish, and a son, Henry, to encourage and support. A family.

"He'll never manage the walk back to your truck." Holly smiled as Henry yawned when Luc lifted him down from the ride.

"Won't have to." A moment later Luc lifted the boy atop his shoulders. Even with all their winnings to carry, Luc managed to capture Holly's hand and hold it. "Did you have fun?"

"It was a wonderful day." The midway's multicolored lights reflected on Holly's face, enhancing her sweet smile. That did funny things to his breathing. "I think Henry enjoyed himself. It was a great send-off for his week away at church camp. It was kind of you to pay for that."

"I heard some kids at church talking about camp. When I asked Henry about it he seemed very keen as long as he could come back to Hilda's after." When they reached the truck, Luc lifted the sleeping boy off his shoulders and into the backseat, then did up his seat belt. Henry barely blinked.

"He's not our little waif anymore," she whispered for Luc's ears only.

"I hope he'll move to the ranch soon. It seems like I've waited forever."

"I'm praying for that." Holly smoothed a hand over Henry's warm sticky cheek, brushing away a fluff of cotton candy.

"Thank you." Slightly surprised that Holly would pray for him, Luc helped her into the truck. "Let's get him home," he said then drove to Hilda's.

Since Hilda was entertaining a friend, Holly offered to put Henry to bed. Luc was only too happy to help.

"Thank you, Luc and Holly," Henry whispered on a big yawn.

"You're welcome, darling. Sleep tight." Holly brushed a featherlight kiss against his brow. Luc copied her actions then paused to gaze at the sleeping boy.

My son. Soon, Lord?

A moment later Holly urged him away to

give Hilda some privacy. Then they were on the road to Holly's.

"Thank you for spending today with me." Luc reached across the seat, holding out his hand for her to grasp.

"It's been my pleasure." She clasped his hand between hers but her gaze was directed out the side window where, now that they'd left town, the stars were clearly visible in the dark sky. "Luc, could I ask you a favor?"

There was a hesitant tone to the question, as if she wasn't quite sure she should have asked.

"Anything," he said quickly. "What do you need, Holly?"

"A friend." She turned and looked at him, her blue eyes filled with shadows. "A really good friend. Please?"

"I'm right here."

As he pulled into her yard, Luc had a sense that tonight would change everything between them.

Maybe it was a dumb thing to do.

Holly knew she should have opened that

trunk months ago and gone through what her dad had left for her on her own. But somehow it always seemed too daunting and she'd put it off. Tonight, with Luc's help, she was going to face whatever was in there.

"Are you sure, Holly?" Luc sat with a glass of iced tea, his gaze intense.

"I'm sure," she whispered. Sitting on the floor in front of the trunk, she crossed her legs, inhaled a breath of courage and leaned forward. Tenderly, she caressed the battered wooden box her father had loved. Then with a swift move she removed the lock, lifted the lid and whispered, "Okay, Dad. What is it you wanted me to find?"

A moment later she was crying.

"Holly—" Luc's hoarse whisper drew her attention. She smiled at him though tears blocked her vision.

"It's okay." Carefully Holly lifted a tiny white infant's dress for Luc to see. "It's mine. Can you imagine he kept it?"

"You were the most precious thing in his life, Holly." Luc came to sit on the floor beside her. As she turned the dress a small blue velvet bag slid out, which he caught. "Look."

Luc upturned the bag. A baby's fragile necklace with a filigree pendant tumbled into his hand. On the back was inscribed *Daughter* with Holly's birth date. Tears burned her throat but Holly swallowed them. There was so much left in the trunk. She couldn't break down now.

"Pictures," she said, pulling out albums she'd never seen before. "I've seen some but—" Her words died at the sight of a woman by her father's side. Her mother. "I must have been about three when they took this. They look happy."

Holly took a sip of her tea and pressed on. Once she'd finished looking at the pictures that followed her all the way through high school, she pulled out the next album. This one featured pictures of every trophy, every award, every achievement she'd ever attained. She had to laugh.

"What's funny?" Luc asked.

"I don't think many of these are worthy of preservation." She chuckled at the photo of herself sitting in a cow paddy, a calf clasped in her young arms.

"I've never seen you look better," Luc teased.

Holly scowled at him before setting the album aside. Next was a copy of the local newspaper. *Holly Janzen wins Buffalo Gap's first full scholarship.* Her chest felt like it was caving in. *Oh, Dad.*

She set that aside with pictures from her high school graduation. *Not much more to go through now*, she told herself. *Nothing to fear.*

"Want to take a break?" Luc asked. When she shook her head, he refilled her tea and waited till she'd taken a sip. "It's not as bad as you thought, is it?"

But a second later it became infinitely worse.

"Toronto Medical College," Luc read from the pamphlet in her hand. "That's your alma mater."

"Yes." Why did her dad have it?

Holly removed a stack of pictures including one of the apartment building where she'd stayed. But her father had never been there. Confused, Holly picked up a brown notebook from the bottom of the box and stared at it. She couldn't read it. Not with Luc here. She was too afraid of what it said. She set it on the floor.

"Holly? What's wrong?" He reached out a hand. Thinking he'd take the book and begin reading, Holly grabbed one corner. A dozen pictures flew across the floor.

Horrified, Holly's gaze slid over them. Guilt covered her in a blanket so thick she almost smothered. But she couldn't stop staring at one tiny beloved face and wondering how her father came to have it.

Luc picked up that picture and studied it for several moments before he frowned at her. "This baby—whose is it, Holly?"

"Mine." She cleared her throat then released the festering secret. "I met a man, Troy, at the church's singles group. I fell in love with him."

"You don't need to tell me, Holly." Luc's arm drew her against his side, his warmth chasing away the chill that crept toward her heart.

"I have to." She clung to the image of her child. "Please, Luc. Can you listen? I've needed to say this for so long."

"Go ahead." Luc tipped up her chin to look into her eyes, his own dark and filled with something soft and wondrous. "I'll listen to whatever you want to tell me. I'm your friend, Holly. I won't judge you."

He would when he heard the whole story. Nevertheless, Holly spoke.

"Troy proposed, said we'd get married after he finished medical school, when he could make enough to buy us a home. I didn't tell Dad. It was so new and—" Holly hung her head as shame suffused her. "I was so gullible. We were getting married. What did it matter if we didn't wait?" She prepared for Luc's condemnation.

"I see." That quiet acceptance meant a great deal to Holly but it didn't expunge her guilt.

"I dumped everything I'd believed in for my entire life to be with this man." She dashed away her tears angrily. "How could I have done that for someone so unworthy?"

"You made a mistake." Luc drew her closer, as if to protect her from herself.

"I sure did. The day I told him I was pregnant, Troy walked out, but only after telling me he thought someone in my profession would have more brains than to get pregnant. I couldn't believe it." She relived her confusion and horror. "A baby, a beautiful blessed baby—and he didn't want it. Or me. He wanted me to have an abortion."

Luc muttered something nasty then. "He was a fool."

"No, I was." Holly caught her breath and poured out the rest. "I knew I couldn't come home or tell Dad."

"But why?" Luc asked, clearly puzzled. "Marcus would have—"

"Been so disappointed in me," she finished wearily. "I was supposed to be an example to kids here that you could have your dreams. I'd received a big scholarship from the town. Everyone knew where I was going and why. They expected me to finish my training and come back, work here, help someone else achieve their dream."

"Holly the local hero." Luc's lips pursed.

"Yes. I couldn't come back with a baby in tow. Besides—" Holly hung her head, unable to say the words.

"They would have known you'd betrayed your Christian principles?" Luc asked.

"Yes." Too ashamed to look at him, she kept her head down. "And that would have reflected badly on Dad as well as me."

"Was your father your primary concern?" Luc's voice held such gentleness.

"Back then I told myself it was, but when I looked back on it, I was protecting myself, too," she admitted. "I didn't want to be the local bad girl. I didn't want anyone gossiping about me or saying nasty things to Dad about me."

"That's natural." Luc's lips rested on her hair for a moment. "So how did you manage?"

"I finished school during my pregnancy. In the summer I told Dad I had to pick up a special course I'd missed, that I'd be home by August." Her heart ached for the lies, half truths, for the phony life she'd led. "I had my baby and I took great pains to make sure he had good solid Christian parents. Then I came home."

"You never told anyone except Ron," he guessed, watching her face. "That was, what—five years later?"

"Yes, about that." Shame weighed her down. "He said he could never be with someone like me who lived a lie. He said I should come clean with the people who believed in me."

"As if that would help anyone." Luc snorted his disgust. "As if he'd have stuck around when the gossip started."

"Ron was right. I should have told them all. It would have been infinitely easier than keeping my secret to myself." Holly gazed down at the tiny innocent face in the picture she held. "But I couldn't do it. I couldn't stand to see Dad's disappointment. He would have been so ashamed of me."

"Marcus Janzen would never have been ashamed of you." Luc shook his head when

Holly twisted to stare at him. His arm tightened around her. His voice was strong when he said, "I think you should read that notebook, Holly. Read it now and learn exactly what your father thought of you."

Holly held her breath, half afraid to know what it said yet needing love so badly.

"Finally, at last, find the truth, Holly," Luc said.

Nodding, she lifted the notebook and began to read. The entire time Luc sat beside her, holding her, encouraging her without words. When she'd gone about a third of the way through the book, she closed it and let the tears stream down her face.

"He came to see me," Holly told him. "He says he was lonely and worried something was wrong."

"That was Marcus." A smile hid in Luc's words.

"He stopped by my apartment and heard that I was in hospital." Holly squeezed her eyes closed. "Someone told me I'd had a visitor," she remembered. "I thought it was Troy, that he wanted our baby. But he'd already left town."

"And your dad?" Luc pressed.

Holly read a little more, groaned and shook her head. "Dad saw his grandchild at the hospital. He said he felt it was my decision and he didn't want to interfere. He was able to give his blessing before the baby was given to his adopted parents. He thanks God for that."

"Marcus saw his grandson, Holly." Luc sounded as shocked as she felt.

"Yes, a perfect little boy whom I could have loved, cared for and taught Dad's values." She closed her eyes as the impact of his words sank deep. "With Dad's support I now know I could have weathered anything Buffalo Gap shot at me, but I gave away that chance. That's why God can't forgive me."

"What?" Luc's fingers tightened on her arm. "Holly, God forgave you long ago."

"How could anyone forgive that?" she asked bitterly.

"Your dad did and so has God. I'm sure if you read further, Marcus never blamed you for your mistake or your decision," Luc insisted. "God has infinitely more compassion to forgive than even your loving earthly father."

"You don't understand." Guilt threatened to crush Holly. Not only had she cheated herself of mothering her child, she'd cheated her father. Her sweet, loving father who'd never said a word about what he'd learned. He'd simply gone on loving her.

"Listen to me." Luc forced her to look at him. "I'm going to adopt Henry, right?"

"Yes." Holly felt confused by his words. "What does that—"

"Let me finish." He cupped her face in his hands, his breath whispering across her face as he spoke. "We both know that sometime in the future, without meaning to, I'm going to make a mistake in raising Henry."

"I think you'll be an awesome father," she said.

"Thank you, darling friend." He pressed a kiss to the end of her nose. "But I'm human. I'll mess up. Do you think God will be able to forgive me for it?"

Holly blinked. "Of course."

"Anything?" Luc pressed. "Will He forgive me anything?"

She thought about it then nodded. "Yes."

"The Bible says He remembers our sins no more. So, my dear Holly, God can forgive me for my mistakes but He can't forgive you for giving away your baby?" Luc shook his head, his eyes tender as his thumbs brushed away her tears. "How big is your God, Holly?"

She'd never thought of it like that. After a moment, Luc released her and shifted to crouch beside her.

"Think about God, Holly. Think on His wonder and His love. God sent His son to die for your sins. All of your sins." Luc stared into her eyes for a long time.

Then he leaned forward and pressed his lips to hers in the sweetest kiss she'd ever received.

"I think you need to read the rest of your father's notebook by yourself. Good night, sweet Holly."

She caught his hand just before he left.

"Thank you." She gathered her courage, feeling her way to the words she wanted, needed to say to him. "You've always been there for me just when I need you most. You're the best friend I've ever had. I love you, Luc."

Luc's dark eyes flared wide. It took him a moment to regroup. He touched her cheek with the tip of one finger and opened his lips as if to respond. Instead, he simply smiled and walked away.

Holly sat far into the night, cradling her father's notebook, reading slowly and reliving the past. Then she bowed her head.

"I told Luc I loved him and he walked away, Daddy." Hot bitter tears burned her cheeks. "How can I ever be enough for him to truly love?"

Chapter Thirteen

I love you, Luc.

Those words had swirled through Luc's brain for days and he still didn't know what to do about them. With Henry away at camp he'd had plenty of time to think about Holly's proclamation and his own response. But thinking didn't help.

"It isn't that I don't love Holly," he spoke aloud as he herded the cattle toward fresh pasture. "I do. I've never been more sure of anything in my life."

Why did he love her? He'd come up with a thousand reasons, but the reason that stuck with Luc most was Holly's gritty determination to protect her father from shame. He loved her for caring so deeply for the man who'd loved her.

"It also makes everything much harder," he told a stubborn steer who wouldn't follow the herd. The steer tilted his head sideways as if he didn't quite understand.

"Don't you get it?" He nudged his horse against the wayward animal. "Something from her past or anything else could come between us. What if she found the baby—it could happen, and then what?"

The very thought of loving Holly and then losing her because of something he hadn't foreseen sent shudders down Luc's back.

"I love her so much. I'd give her every bit of love I have to give," he whispered. "But if it wasn't enough, if something happened, I'd never be whole again."

It sounded silly and overly dramatic but experiencing love with Holly only to later lose it would be his mortal wound.

That would be unbearable.

Satisfied that the herd was now safely ensconced in a new feeding area, Luc rode home. He prayed for courage to accept this love and leave the future to God, but his fear drowned out his prayers. Did that mean God intended for him to concentrate on his goal of building his ranch? Was that God's will?

Luc had barely unsaddled his horse when a noise alerted him to someone else's presence. Holly stood by the barn door still clad in her work scrubs, her face pale but brimming with determination.

"Do you have time to talk?" she asked in a quiet voice.

"Sure. Come on in, I'll make coffee." Luc modulated his too-jovial tone. "How are you, Holly?"

"Confused." Instead of going into his house, she sat down on the old willow bench under a huge birch tree whose leaves trembled in the breeze.

"Oh?" he pretended nonchalance.

"I've been trying to understand why you've stayed away." Her troubled gaze held his. "You're probably disgusted by what I told you but—"

"Holly, stop." Luc sat on the grass in front of her and took her hands. "I'm not disgusted. I'm only sad you had to go through it all."

"Oh." Was that relief on her face?

"You don't deserve punishment. You've punished yourself enough." Luc squeezed her hands then let go of them because the contact caused too much inner turmoil and he needed to concentrate on what he had to say. "God doesn't hold grudges. He's forgiven you. The past is over. It's time to move on."

"But I told you—"

"I can't love you, Holly." Her shoulders sagged and her eyes misted, and for a moment Luc wished he'd never said those words.

"Why?"

"Because at heart I'm a coward. I refuse to risk loving and losing." Luc hated revealing his weakness but he needed her to stop believing there could be anything between them.

"Can you explain that?" Holly asked, and when he didn't immediately respond she leaned closer. "Please? I need to understand."

He'd give anything to erase the pain from her eyes.

Anything but love.

"I couldn't take it in when my parents died," Luc began. "I had no relatives to soften the loss. My world crashed and nobody explained anything to me." He still felt the fear lingering in the deepest recesses of his soul. "Everything was bewildering. I'd been happy at home, but, suddenly that was gone. My parents were gone. My life was gone and all I knew was that it would never be the same again."

"Oh, Luc." Her empathy forced him to continue.

"The social workers tried," he said, "but I ended up being shunted from place to place with no say about where I stayed, with whom or for how long."

"That's why you identify with Henry," Holly said.

"I guess." Luc shrugged. "Anyway, one thing kept me going." He felt his body tense as he prepared to reveal his own dark secret. "I had this dream that one day I'd make a place of my own, control my own future. Then I'd finally be home and safe."

"So you bought your ranch." The way Holly said that made it sound so easy.

"I did. But it took a long time and a lot of determination." He fell silent, loath to replay what he'd endured to make his dream live.

"Tell me, Luc." Her soft, cajoling words drew the past from his lips.

"I needed a lot of money so I chose the oil fields. Labor is always in demand there and they pay well, if you can stick it out. I did." He tried to conceal his shudder by shifting on the grass. "I chose the least favorite, highest paid shifts, I accepted the dirtiest job with danger pay and endured the most abusive bosses to earn top dollar for every hour. I dragged myself to bed every night wondering if I'd make it up again in the morning and then rise wondering if anyone would notice if I didn't."

Holly watched him without saying a word. She'd crossed her legs beneath her, huddling against the bench as he spoke.

"But I couldn't make money fast enough."

Luc squeezed his eyes closed. "I craved a place of my own. That's why I started fighting. For money. A lot of money."

"Oh." Holly blinked as if she didn't quite understand. "You never said this before."

"It's not something I'm very proud of." He forced a smile. "I want to make my mark, Holly. I want people to know I was here on this earth. I wanted to create a legacy for my child so that he would never have to feel as lost and alone as I did."

"There's nothing wrong with that," she defended.

"Maybe not but I got consumed by my goals. So every weekend off I headed to Calgary and took on another competitor. And every time I won. I was willing to risk any injury if it meant more money. I kept going to build my savings account no matter what." Did she think that was silly? She who'd always belonged?

"You were hurt?" she asked. Luc nodded.

"Many times. Sometimes I almost didn't make it to work. I didn't care. I just kept punching my way to enough cash to finally leave the rigs and the fighting." Luc looked away but somehow he needed to see Holly's reaction so he lifted his head and stared at her. "I have a lot of scars from those years and a lot of bad memories. Like you with your baby, I don't talk about it."

She nodded, her eyes brimming with understanding. Luc had never loved her more.

"Now I have my ranch." He couldn't look at her now, not when he was going to refuse her love. "This is the only place I've felt secure since my parents died."

"And loving me puts that at risk?" She frowned at his nod. "How? We could combine our ranches, make something truly spectacular that we could both be proud of. If you could let go of your fear, we could trust God to give us a wonderful future."

Holly went on, listing opportunities Luc yearned to develop, suggesting ways that together made them stronger.

"I love Henry as much as you do, Luc," she said. "I think I could be a good mother."

"You would be a fantastic mother." He said it without hesitation, a mental image of

Holly and Henry laughing together filling his mind. For a moment he wavered. Maybe it was possible. Maybe they could…

Luc's cell phone rang. He glanced at Holly, who smiled.

"Go ahead and answer it. I'll wait."

"Thanks." His heart sank at the sound of his buddy Andy's voice. He'd just received divorce papers. "Can I call you right back?" Luc asked. He hung up, glanced at Holly. "I'm sorry, Holly. I wish I had it in me to take a chance on a future with you, but I just can't jeopardize my future. What's happened to him—" he inclined his head toward his phone "—could happen to us and it terrifies me. If I could marry anyone, Holly, it would be you. But I can't risk it."

"You mean you won't." She rose, her back very straight.

"Yes."

"If you really believe that placing our faith in God to help us keep a relationship together would be a risk then you shouldn't do it," she said, her voice cool and calm. "You've talked a lot about finding God's will for your life.

I'd never say I'm God's will for you, but I do believe that you will never discover His plan for you until you free yourself of the fear that loving someone means your world will come crashing down around you."

Luc knew she was hurting. Because of him. He rose slowly, held out a hand. "Holly, I wish—"

"Don't wish anymore, Luc. You've been granted your wish in this ranch. Soon you'll have Henry, too. I hope you enjoy both." She walked away from him in a dignified stride, head held high.

Luc watched her ride away, his hands clenched. Every cell in his body wanted to run after her, to gather her in his arms and hang on forever. But he couldn't do that.

He'd just have to learn how to be content with his life without Holly.

Somehow.

"I'm sorry, sweetie, but I don't know how to help you." Three weeks later, Abby hugged Holly. "Luc has to find his security in God's time. You can't force it."

"I know. It's just so hard, living so close. How am I going to go on seeing him every day, pretending we're only friends?" Holly sipped the hot strong coffee Abby had served and tried not to envy her friend her happy marriage, darling twins and adopted son, Ivor. Abby's life was full while Holly's felt so empty.

"You're going to leave Luc to God. He's the only one who can work it out." Abby smiled. "Maybe it's time to try something new."

Holly thought about Abby's advice all the way home. There she surveyed her work-room with its shelves now stocked full of many sweet outfits, just waiting for online orders. Try something new, but what? All she wanted was Luc.

She made herself a salad then later took Melody for a short ride, careful to avoid areas where she thought Luc might be. Though August's wane and the shift to September's autumn was her favorite season, Holly found little solace in the ride. All she could think of was that now the freedom she'd always found on Cool Springs Ranch was gone. From this point on it would be very uncomfortable to work with Luc as her foreman.

His declaration still haunted her. Gentle Luc a fighter? She couldn't wrap her mind around it. It had been so unexpected. So had his rejection. Now she felt exposed and on edge whenever she was in town, worried she'd run into Luc. When she didn't get that glimpse she craved, she was certain her feelings for him were obvious to everyone. Her situation became more untenable when Mayor Marsha and others asked questions about their relationship.

"Luc and I are friends, Mayor." Holly laughed in her most carefree voice. "Always have been. You know that."

She didn't want friendship. Holly wanted his love, which he wouldn't give. Day after day she champed at the bit, increasingly unsatisfied by a job she'd always loved. For weeks she prayed for a way to find peace until one night she sat on the deck studying September's full moon and relinquished her dreams.

"Okay, God," she huffed at last. "I give up. I can't do anything about Luc. You are the only one who can heal his past. I love him but I'm leaving him up to You. I can't change my mistakes but with Your help I'm letting go of the guilt and my struggle to be perfect Holly. Please show me *Your* plan for my future."

It felt good to say those words, to stop striving to be what she was not. It also hurt beyond belief to accept that God's will might not include a relationship with Luc.

Chilled by the night air, Holly returned inside the house to clean up the kitchen. Maybe that would keep her mind busy. While wiping the counters a piece of paper fell on the floor. Holly bent to pick it up. Her eyes widened.

Suddenly she knew what to do. She made the call that would change her life and take her away from Luc Cramer.

Though he was a wonderful man, he just wasn't for her.

Feeling dog-tired, Luc slid off his horse, onto a stone by the creek and exhaled. These past weeks he'd thrown himself into work from the earliest morning hours to far beyond midnight, trying to chase away the memory of Holly's shattered face. It didn't work.

Every waking moment he saw again her disappointment in him. In between, he remembered the sad looks she gave him when she thought he wasn't watching. If they occasionally met, she thrust out her chin and held his gaze, but Luc saw the pain lurking in those beautiful blue eyes.

Henry was their buffer. With Henry, Holly almost returned to the smiling woman Luc had always admired. With Luc, Holly was cool and businesslike.

"Why doesn't Holly like you?" Henry kept asking.

She loves me. But I'm afraid to love her.

Since Luc couldn't say that, he changed the subject. But often Henry's dark eyes rested on him, brimming with questions. All Luc wanted was the old Holly back, the one who carried her heart on her sleeve.

The one he'd hurt.

"Luc?"

He startled, almost dropped the soda he'd pulled from his saddle pack. Holly stood in front of him, eyes shadowed by her white Stetson.

"Holly." His voice came out hoarse. Luc cleared his throat before asking, "How are you?"

"I need to talk to you." She looked so lovely with the sun blazing down on a shirt that perfectly matched her eyes. He wanted to—

"Go ahead." He waved to a nearby stone but Holly shook her head.

"Are you still interested in buying Cool Springs Ranch?" she asked in a chilly not-like-Holly voice.

Luc's jaw dropped. Never in a million scenarios had he envisioned this.

"I'm moving to Calgary," she said, filling the gap his lack of speech left. "I've accepted a position at the hospital there. I'll be leaving next week."

Luc couldn't take it in. It didn't make sense. Holly loved the ranch, treasured every square mile of the place her father had cared for.

"Why?" he asked.

"Because I've spent too many years trying to be something I'm not. Because I've let guilt for giving away my baby steal years of my life." Her voice, which had started out strong and defiant, gave way to a wobble. She cleared her throat. "Because I won't waste any more time wishing you would take a chance with me on love."

"Holly—"

"I'm starting fresh in Calgary. I intend to find new ways for God to use me. I refuse to be anyone's role model or pretend to be anyone but who God created." Finally, she added, "I can't stay in Buffalo Gap anymore."

"But your dad worked years to build up Cool Springs just for you." Luc shook his head. "How can you just walk away?"

"That was his dream. Besides, he'd understand my decision." Her voice softened as she looked across the land. "He only ever wanted me to be the best I can." Her gaze shifted to Luc. "Dad's in my heart, meshed in my memories."

Luc marveled at the determined undertone in her voice.

"The ranch is just a thing. It's the people in my life who are important." She waved a hand. "I'm offering a lease with the possibility of a sale. I want to concentrate on where God's taking me. I won't have time to fret about this place."

Holly said the words but Luc could see the effort it cost her.

"I'm not the town mascot or its ambassador or any of those other silly things I've tried to live up to. I'm Holly Janzen and I love you, Luc Cramer." Her blue gaze met his with unblinking directness. "But I refuse to hang around here pining over what will never be. This is your chance to complete your empire. You'll finally have your dream."

Luc struggled for words and failed. Holly smiled as if she understood.

"All I ask is that you keep the sale quiet until I've left town. You can talk to my lawyer about the details." She waited for him to respond, but Luc was still processing. Holly stepped forward, brushed her lips against his cheek and said, "Goodbye, Luc."

Then she swung onto Melody and rode away.

And took Luc's heart with her.

Chapter Fourteen

Holly shoved her dad's beloved trunk into her vehicle then surveyed the ranch one last time. She'd already said goodbye to her horses, her friends, Henry, her life. There was nothing left to do but leave.

"You would have understood, wouldn't you, Dad?" she said as she drove the familiar road away from what had always been home. "Just as you wouldn't have been ashamed or hurt by my baby. You would have forgiven me and welcomed my child into our family. I should have known that."

She should have known her friends would have done the same. She should have trusted them enough. Regrets that she'd lost her baby still stung. They probably always would. But thanks to her father Holly had the precious baby pictures to help her heal. She'd also found ammunition against her guilt. The knowledge that her baby was in God's hands and He was the best father any child could have. Her job was to walk the new path He'd set her on.

And yet the future looked bittersweet to Holly. Until she remembered the promises she'd read this morning from Isaiah's fifty-eighth chapter:

The Lord will always lead you. He will satisfy your needs in dry lands and give strength to your bones. You will be like a garden that has much water, like a spring that never runs dry.

"Yes, I will, God," she said firmly.

There was the old maple tree in whose crook Luc had found her the day Ron dumped her. And there was the paddock where he'd helped her rescue Henry from Ornery Joe. There was the hill where Luc had lit fireworks last New Year's Eve because her father was too sick to do it and the meadow where she'd hoped they would both teach Henry barrel racing and gymkhana. Holly drove slowly, savoring every detail.

This was where she'd found love and lost it.

"Thank You for these precious memories," she whispered. They were dear—that's why she couldn't stay here, couldn't see Luc every day and know he didn't love her enough to overcome his fears. "My heart hurts, God, but I trust You to work all things to Your good."

This was the hardest day of trust she'd ever had.

"I don't want to go to the creek," Henry said, a mutinous look in his eyes. "It's not fun without Holly."

No, it wasn't. Nothing was, Luc freely admitted. Nothing had been fun since Holly had left two weeks ago.

"What *do* you want to do today?" he asked, regretting his own grumpy tone.

"Nothin'." Henry slumped down, not even interested in Sheba's puppies.

Luc's fingers itched to call Holly and ask her advice. In fact, he even pulled out his phone but never dialed, fear stopping him. A second later it rang.

"Is it Holly?" Henry asked eagerly when Luc answered.

Luc shook his head then told Abby to continue. What she said made his blood run cold.

"I don't know how but Shelly has managed to convince her supervisors that Henry is not thriving here. They have rescinded his case from me back to Shelly," Abby said, obviously disgruntled. "Shelly advised them that Henry will be better off in a family with two parents rather than with a single dad. She's already found an interested couple."

"Meaning?" Luc needed Abby to spell it out.

"At this point, your adoption of Henry is off."

Luc listened blankly to her reassurances, said the right things and eventually hung up.

No, God, his soul cried, but he could say

nothing. Shelly had insisted Henry was not to know until she told him.

"What's wrong, Luc?" Henry asked as if sensing his world had just shifted. His small hand slipped inside Luc's. He whispered, "I won't be cranky anymore."

"Oh, Henry. I love you." Luc hunched down and gathered this beloved child into his arms while his heart screamed "Why?"

"I love you, too, Luc." Henry hugged him back but after a moment wiggled free. "Too tight."

Luc laughed though his heart was breaking.

"Let's roast some hot dogs for lunch," he said, knowing that would please Henry. "Then we'll have to get you home. Ms. Hilda's going to get you some new clothes for school."

"'Cause I'm getting big," Henry boasted, his chest puffed out. "I wish Holly could see me growing."

"I do, too, son." The endearment stung. Henry was never going to be his son.

Luc did his best to make the meal fun for

Henry but as he drove home from Hilda's later a pall settled over him.

Hoping to shake it, he saddled his horse and rode the ranch hills. All this would be his. It was the legacy he'd worked for but now it was meaningless. It was just land, a house, a ranch. There was no security here. Life had side-swiped him and he was alone. There was no way to protect himself.

This is your chance to complete your empire. You'll finally have your dreams.

Holly's words rang in his ears. But his dream hadn't been to own land. That was just the path he'd chosen to attain what he most wanted—to belong, to love and be loved.

For the second time that day Luc's phone rang.

"Hey, buddy," said his friend Andy. "I'm at your ranch. You said we'd have a steak barbecue tonight, remember? Where are you?"

"On the way." Luc turned his horse and headed for home, dreading the thought of entertaining tonight. He had nothing to offer Andy or anyone else.

As it turned out, Andy was good company. He talked a lot about his kids and though that hurt Luc because he couldn't stop thinking of Henry, it didn't seem to bother Andy.

When dark had fallen they sat outside by the fire pit, coffee mugs in hand as they stared into the coals. The fire encouraged intimacy so Luc finally asked the question that had plagued him for months.

"Are you ever sorry you got married?"

"Are you kidding?" Andy showed his astonishment. "I'd have missed everything. Being a husband, loving a good woman, being a dad. I could never regret that."

"But you've been so hurt," Luc pointed out.

"So? I was hurt when you fought me, remember? But I never regretted the pain when I made that hefty house payment." Andy leaned back, a tiny smile lifting his lips.

"Which you've now lost," Luc pointed out.

"Nope. It's still protecting my family. Besides, I'm not sure all's lost. I believe God's working since I stopped trying to force things and let Him be in control. Finally fig-

ured out all I have to do is take the opportunities He gives me."

"Things are better for you, then?"

"We're talking is all. But that's a big
step from two months ago." Andy glanced
around. "Hey, where's Holly? I thought for
sure she'd stop by."

"She moved to Calgary." Suddenly, without
meaning to, Luc was pouring out the whole
sad story. When he finished, he waited, hoping for some sympathy, maybe a little advice.
He didn't expect derision.

"Are you nuts?" Andy gaped at him. "This
gorgeous, smart, funny woman tells you she
loves you and you chicken out from life?'

"You only met her once," Luc reminded.
"In passing."

"So? I recognize quality when I see it,"
Andy shot back. "Do you love her?"

"Of course, but—"

"There are no buts, buddy. My marital
problems have taught me one thing. Love is
what life's about. People die, disappoint or
leave. Love is the only thing that endures."
Andy waved a hand. "One day this place will

be gone and you'll be forgotten by everyone but the ones who loved you. Who will that be if you don't reach out and accept when love is offered you?"

"I can't," he said forcefully.

"You can't what? Take the love God offered you for an amazing woman who would share every aspect of your life on this ranch?" Andy shook his head. "Do you know how rare real love is? Instead of opening your heart to such an incredible gift, you let fear take over. You chose your ranch over her. What else is she going to do but pack up and leave?"

"I never thought about it that way," Luc mumbled.

"So think about it. You've got this magnificent spread, your dream. But Holly's gone and Henry will be soon. What's left? What good is your beloved dream if you can't share it?"

There was nothing to say. Andy was right and Luc knew it. But how could he be sure he wasn't making a mistake?

"All this time, I should have taken my own

advice because you're not qualified on love, Luc." Andy was only half joking. He rose and dumped out his coffee. "Think and pray about it, buddy. This is a turning point in your faith journey. You've got to trust God sometime." After a slap on the shoulder and a "thanks for supper," Andy left.

Luc sat alone in the darkness with only the faint wail of coyotes.

"So what do I do? What is Your will?"

But he knew. Inside he knew God's will.

God had gifted him with love for Holly and Henry. Whether or not that love would flourish into something he'd only ever dreamed of was not the question. The question was whether or not he'd throw it away.

"What in the world?" Holly blinked groggily. Two thirty in the morning and someone was banging on her door as if there was a fire.

The banging stopped for two seconds then resumed even louder.

"I'm coming," she called as she tied the belt of her robe. "Please stop making that racket," she begged as she dragged open the door then gasped. "Luc? What's wrong?"

"Everything." He leaned against the door frame, tall, lean and incredibly handsome even in the greenish glare of a cheap light fixture. "I need to talk to you."

All down the hallway doors opened and necks craned to see the cause of the commotion. Holly knew that tomorrow she'd get a call from the super to complain about the noise. How she hated this compacted living; she missed the freedom of Cool Springs Ranch.

"You have to talk to me in the middle of the night?" she snapped, irritated by the lack of privacy from curious onlookers. "Well, you can't stand out here to do it. Come in." She latched onto his arm and tugged him inside her apartment. "Now," she demanded, hands on her hips, "what is so important that it couldn't—"

Luc's lips covered hers in a kiss that reached into her heart and pulled her into the circle of his strong arms, right where she'd longed to be. Holly kissed him back, her lips molded to his, her arms sliding around his neck as she wordlessly told him what lay in her heart. How could she not? She'd lived, prayed for this moment. Now she asked no questions, simply gloried in the relief of expressing her love for this magnificent, attractive, delightfully frustrating man.

At last, breathless, Holly eased back to study Luc's beloved face, so glad he kept his strong muscular arms tight around her waist.

"I love you, Holly," Luc said, his voice hushed, reverent. "I have forever but I was afraid to say it. You are what gives my world meaning. You give me strength and support. Without you nothing matters and that scares me a whole lot more than loving you. Come home where you belong, Holly. Please?"

Her smile began with his first words and grew wider the longer he spoke. When he finally finished, she couldn't hide her joy any longer. It spurted out of her in a bubble of laughter.

"Oh, Luc. You really are Mr. Just In Time, aren't you?" She pressed her lips against his mouth once more then broke off the kiss to draw him forward.

"I asked you a question," Luc said with a frown.

"Which I intend to answer. Come and sit down, darling, and I'll explain."

"I like the darling part," he murmured in her ear before following her across the room. Once he was seated on her knobby sofa, Holly sat beside him, deliriously happy when he lifted his arm to draw her close against his side. She left his embrace for one second to lean forward and lift a paper from the coffee table.

"What's that?" He broke away from caressing her neck to stare curiously at the paper.

"This, my darling Luc, is a deal I made with God." She smiled at his mystified look. "It's a lease agreement. You had until tomorrow, technically today," she reminded him, "to contact me before I sign it for a year's lease on this place. For saving me from that alone you deserve many thanks."

"So thank me," he said with a twinkle in his dark eyes. So Holly thanked him as best she could in a kiss that came from her heart and needed no words to explain. "Surely you wouldn't have stayed here?" he asked sometime later with a disapproving glance around. "It's so—" he paused, searching for the right word.

"Ugly?" Holly supplied, hiding her smile.

"Exactly. And this sofa is about as comfortable as the rocks at the creek."

"How I've missed that creek," she told him.

"Then let's go." Luc rose and reached out for her hand.

"Luc, we can't go to the creek now." Holly let him draw her into his arms anyway.

"Work?" he asked, brushing his lips across her forehead.

"No, I'm off tomorrow but—"

"Come on, Holly," he murmured before kissing her once more. "At least come for a ride with me. Please?"

How could she withstand that loving, tender voice? She couldn't. Five minutes later she was changed and riding toward Buffalo Gap in his restored truck. The moments seemed too special, too precious to spend talking so Holly sat next to Luc, silently savoring the joy of having this beloved man of her dreams so near. It seemed mere moments before they arrived at Cool Springs Ranch.

"You've saddled Melody," she marveled when he helped her from the truck. Luc cupped his hands, offering her a step to mount the horse. Then he swung up onto his own.

"Let's go," Luc invited. Holly nodded.

The September night was clear with a blazingly bright full moon that lit their way up the hills to the spot Holly treasured most. She'd never thought to return and now caught her breath at the beauty of the silver-sparkled water, the milky white stones glowing in the moonlight and the murmur of bubbling creek water.

"Look, Holly," Luc whispered, one arm around her waist while the other waved to the panoramic view before them. "This is our land. This is our home."

"Yours," she corrected.

Luc shook his head.

"Ours." He helped her sit on the largest boulder then knelt in front of her. "Before he died, your father made me promise that I'd make sure you were happy. I haven't done a very good job of that. I'd like to make amends starting now."

"Oh, Luc." She loved his hands covering hers then linking their fingers together.

"I love you, Holly. Without you, nothing else in my world matters." Luc's voice betrayed no pause, no hesitation. "I'm sorry I never told you that. I'm sorry I didn't make sure you knew that you are my security, my meaning, the one I trust above all others."

"I love you, too, Luc," she whispered. "So much."

He smiled but placed a finger against her lips letting her know he needed to say this.

"This love for you is the most precious gift God's ever given me. It allows me to face the future with you with no fear, because God will be behind us. It means I can handle anything as long as God is with us."

Holly studied his dear face with misty eyes and a heart full of praise. Once again God had proven his love for her by sending her this beloved man.

"What I'm asking you for, Holly, is a life partnership, a non-breakable promise that I will hold you to," he warned, his voice tense. "I need you to love me as much as I love you."

For a moment the world around them stood still, breathless, waiting. Then,

"Will you marry me, Holly Janzen?"

"On one condition," she said through her tears.

"Name it." Luc held her gaze, hands and voice steady.

"You can't rescind it," she said, tenderly cupping his face in her hands. "You can't ever take it back. I love you, Luc Cramer. Since that's not going to change, this has to be a lifetime commitment."

They solemnly shook on it, laughed gleefully then sealed the deal in the most satisfactory way possible—a kiss. When Luc finally released her, Holly asked about Henry.

"The adoption's fallen through," Luc told her, holding her tight as if to stave off the pain. He explained what Abby had told him. "He's not going to be our son."

"You're going to have to be tougher if you intend to stick with me, Luc." Holly held him close. "We have God on our side and He is faithful. He led the three of us together that first morning when we found Henry. He's not going to abandon us now. This is our first hurdle and we'll trust God. Agreed?"

"How could God have blessed me with such a smart intelligent woman?" Luc asked after he'd sealed their agreement with a kiss.

"Because He's God and He knew you needed me," she shot back with a grin.

"Thank You, Lord." They sat side by side on the rocks, talking, sharing everything in their hearts as the first streaks of daylight turned the sky peach.

"I meant to tell you, Holly. I'm not buying your ranch." Luc smiled at her immediate protest. "Now who doesn't have faith?"

"Tell me your plan." She leaned against him and listened.

"We'll run them as equal partners," Luc

told her. "That's if you want to come back to the ranch. What about your new job?"

"I'm supposed to work a month before deciding but I'd already decided to give notice. I realized it's not where God wants me." She chuckled. "I was waiting to learn His next step but I didn't think I'd find out in the wee hours. Now I know it's with you and Henry. Want to hear *my* plan?"

While the sun crested over the hills, Holly laid out her plan to adopt Henry and then to take online training so she'd be able to help more women.

"I'm going to ask Abby to let me add a counseling service to Family Ties to help those ladies who need us." She raised an eyebrow for Luc's input.

"Just keep some time free for your husband," he said to which she readily agreed.

Chapter Fifteen

"Luc, you're not going to make it back in time for our wedding," Holly wailed into the phone one late-October morning.

"You're not getting out of marrying me," he said, puffing slightly. "Even if I was late, you know very well it would be worth it."

"So what happened?" she asked, breathless with anticipation at the way her life was changing.

"Your judge heard we're getting married today, asked me about Shelly's petition then told me how much he'd appreciated your nursing ability when he had his heart attack. I told him about our great relationship with Henry and Finn and that we are the best couple the two of them could ever have as parents." He chuckled. "He told me how grateful he was to have you when he was in hospital, and—"

"Luc, get to the point," Holly said with a quick glance at the clock in her bedroom.

"He signed our adoption petition. We are Henry's parents."

Unable to contain her joy, she let out a scream. Then she heard the sound of the phone falling and a faraway squeak of dismay coming from Luc.

"Luc?"

He was going to be late coming back from Calgary. Holly just knew it. And then the release of the birds would be off, which would annoy Mayor Marsha whose idea it was. And that would annoy the school bandleader who wanted his group to perform a "bird" song as Marsha's birds took flight, which in turn would—

"Holly? Holly, are you there?" Luc was back on the phone. "You're worrying again, aren't you?"

"I can't help it, Luc. I love them all but

they've taken our simple wedding in the meadow and turned it into some kind of Buffalo Gap circus. And now you're going to be late."

"Impossible. I'm almost to your place. You better be ready to go. I love you, Holly." Luc hung up.

Holly sniffed, clicked off the phone, adjusted her Stetson and the white wedding dress she'd made and decorated with her favorite lace then went to open the door. In the distance she could see dust trails from Luc's restored truck. He'd pick her up then they'd ride to the meadow where they'd be married in front of anyone from Buffalo Gap who wanted to attend. Which by now was probably every one of them.

"'This is the day that the Lord hath made,'" she recited between calming breaths as Luc finally pulled up. She slid into his arms for a reassuring kiss. "Darling, your truck looks magnificent with those ribbons."

"That was Hilda's idea. She wants to make wedding knots or something. I sure hope she doesn't leave any scratches." Luc

leaned back to survey her. "You're beautiful, Holly. A credit to the town, best bride
Buffalo Gap's ever seen, symbol of everything—" He had to stop because Holly put
her hand over his mouth.

"In about ten minutes, if you don't delay,
I will be Holly Cramer and I'll never have
to pay attention to what anyone says about
Holly Janzen again," she told him. "Now
let's go."

"Huh." Luc helped her into the truck then
climbed in beside her. "Is my name the only
reason you're marrying me?"

"Not even close," Holly assured him with
a smug smile.

After a very satisfying embrace, which de-
layed the wedding a little longer, they drove
to the meadow where Henry waited impa-
tiently.

"What's around your neck, Henry?" Luc
asked, shooting Holly a surprised look. She
shook her head.

"I'm the ring bearer, right?" Henry glanced
at them, waiting for reassurance.

"Right." Holly bent and pressed a kiss

against his cheek. "Everyone will know that because you're carrying a pillow with our rings."

"Yeah. And everybody knows Luc. But you went away," Henry said to Holly. He shoved his glasses up his nose with one hand, his little face as serious as could be. "So me an' Tommy, my buddy from school, hafta make sure all these people know who you are."

"Good idea." Luc winked at Holly.

"So we made a sign to tell them." As Henry shifted a sign swung from his back to his front. "We did it at school. Teacher helped us to not spell it wrong."

Here comes the bride.

Holly wasn't sure whether to laugh or cry. All she knew was this precious boy and man were hers to love forever. Because God so loved her.

"All right now." Luc's arm slid around her waist. "Are we ready to get married, Holly?"

Just then Ornery Joe stuck his head through a nearby grove of trees. Holly glanced at Luc.

"Really?"

"A lesson in getting softened by love would do him good." Luc kissed her nose. "Don't worry, he can't get out."

"Make that a three-ring circus," Holly muttered.

"Which you love." Luc leaned toward her. "Ready?"

"Absolutely."

Luc signaled to Hilda, who attached the rings to Henry's pillow then urged him down the makeshift aisle, his sign bumping from knee to knee as he walked. Luc hurried around the side of the assembled townsfolk to the arch in front and waited beside Pastor Don for Holly.

Holly paused to take in the blessings God had showered on her. Everything in her life had led her to this moment. She could not regret any of it.

"I love you, Dad," she whispered inside her heart. Then she took the next step to the rest of her life.

* * * * *

Dear Reader,

Welcome back to my fictional town of Buffalo Gap where cowboys roam as freely as their herds. I hope you enjoyed Holly and Luc's story. Holly is trying to live up to the town's high expectations and Luc has never quite been able to let go of the loss of his family and security. Neither is ready to let go of the past and move into what God has specially planned for them until they relinquish their lack of trust in the Father who is love. Their story reminds us that none of us stands alone, each of us requires God's grace, leading and forgiveness before we can truly live as His children. Henry is a reminder that though life is rarely simple it can be filled with simple joy if we will trust.

I love to hear from readers. You can friend me at facebook.com/LoisRicherAuthor, via email at loisricher@yahoo.com or through loisricher.com. For those who prefer snail mail, you can write to me at Box 639, Nipawin, Sk. Canada S0E 1E0.

Till we meet again I pray you'll feel the intense, never-ending, gloriously motivating love of our Father God in every aspect of your life.

Blessings,

Lois Richer